Three Astral: Thought's Deception

# OrangeBooks Publication

1st Floor, Rajhans Arcade, Mall Road, Kohka, Bhilai, Chhattisgarh 490020

Website: **www.orangebooks.in**

---

**© Copyright, 2024, Author**

All rights reserved. No part of this book may be reproduced, stored in a retrieval system, or transmitted, in any form by any means, electronic, mechanical, magnetic, optical, chemical, manual, photocopying, recording or otherwise, without the prior written consent of its writer.

**First Edition, 2024**

**ISBN:** 978-93-6554-148-9

# THREE ASTRAL

## THOUGHT'S DECEPTION

## TATHASTU

**OrangeBooks Publication**
www.orangebooks.in

# Instructions for Reading "Three Astral – Thought Deception"

Welcome to "Three Astral - Thought Deception," an immersive and unique reading experience that alternates between the worlds of Earth and Three Astral. This book is designed to provide a rich, layered narrative by interweaving chapters from Tathastu's life on Earth and his experiences as Kenyzee on Three Astral. To fully appreciate the story, please follow these instructions:

## Middle Part of the Book
Start by reading the middle part chapters to understand the essential background and context.

## Left Side/Earth-based Chapters
These chapters focus on Tathastu's life on Earth, his struggles with seizures, and the unfolding mystery of his connection to Three Astral.

## Right Side/Three Astral-based Chapters
These chapters delve into the adventures of Kenyzee on the planet Three Astral, exploring its mysteries and challenges.

# Navigation

### Middle Part Of The Book

Chapter - 1 The Origin ..................................................... **116**

Chapter - 2 Formation Of Earth ........................................ **119**

Chapter - 3 The Formation Of Three Astral Planet ............. **124**

Chapter - 4 The Role Of Core Elements ............................. **129**

Chapter - 5 The Elemental Harmonizers ........................... **133**

Chapter - 6 The Threat Of Dark Matter ............................. **135**

Chapter - 7 Solution To Tackle Dark Matter ...................... **138**

*Turn To Chapter 1: Left Hand Side (Page no. 2)*


### Left Side/Earth-Based Chapters

Chapter - 1 Just A Boring Life ............................................... **2**

Chapter - 2 Interests And Observations ............................... **7**

Chapter - 3 First Seizure ..................................................... **13**

Chapter - 4 Weird Feelings And Incidents Post-Seizure ........ **22**

Chapter - 5 Discovery Of Jikoya .......................................... **32**

Chapter - 6 Risk In The Dark Web ....................................... **41**

Chapter - 7 Solution To Tackle Dark Matter ....................... **50**

*Turn To Chapter 1: Right Hand Side (Page no. 144)*

Chapter - 8 Awakening Back To Normal Post Jikoya Effects ................................................. **55**

Chapter - 9 Deeper Hallucinations ....................................... **65**

Chapter - 10 Finally Taking The Drug Again To Understand The Connection ............................................... **73**

*Turn To Chapter 7: Right Hand Side (Page no. 196)*

Chapter - 11 Hospitalization And Realizations ..................... **81**

Chapter - 12 Sister Helps Me Get That Drug ........................ **91**

*Turn To Chapter 11: Right Hand Side (Page no. 230)*

Chapter - 13 Dream End, Tried Jikoya But Can't See Anything ........................................................................ **96**

Chapter - 14 Back To Home ............................................... **102**

Chapter - 15 Final Move ..................................................... **108**

*Turn To Chapter 15: Right Hand Side (Page no. 268)*

Chapter - 16 Real Truth ...................................................... **110**

## Right Side/Three Astral-Based Chapters

Chapter - 1 Arrival On Three Astral .................................... **144**

Chapter - 2 Hijoka And? ..................................................... **150**

Chapter - 3 Meeting With Lika ........................................... **156**

Chapter - 4 Journey To The Green Core Element ............... **162**

Chapter - 5 Introduction To Greenions (Midori) ................ **174**

Chapter - 6 Journey To The Renions' Region (Kaji) And The Snonions' Region (Kori) ........................................ **183**

***Turn To Chapter 8: Left Hand Side (Page no. 55)***

Chapter - 7 Resume Dream ............................................... **196**

Chapter - 8 Formation Of G-Four Astral ............................ **204**

Chapter - 9 Confused ...................................................... **218**

Chapter - 10 Lika Lost Everything .................................... **224**

***Turn To Chapter 11: Left Hand Side (Page no. 81)***

Chapter - 11 Developing Friendship With Lika................... **230**

Chapter - 12 Training With Riko (Harmonizer)................... **239**

Chapter - 13 Learning From Airi And Mentor Tira.............. **249**

Chapter - 14 It Started .................................................... **262**

***Turn To Chapter 13: Left Hand Side (Page no. 96)***

Chapter - 15 I Made It..................................................... **268**

***Turn To Chapter 16: Left Hand Side (Page no. 110)***

*Three Astral: Thought's Deception*

# Left Side/Earth-Based Chapters

## Chapter - 1
# Just a Boring Life

***Watching the World Go By***

I sat in the shadow of a large, old tree that stood at the edge of the school playground. Its branches stretched out wide, providing a cool, shady refuge from the blazing afternoon sun. From my spot, I had a clear view of the playground, where my schoolmates were engaged in their usual activities. The girls were playing their girly games—some were skipping rope, their laughter echoing through the air, while others were involved in a game of hopscotch, diligently hopping from one square to another. Their bright smiles and carefree attitudes seemed to paint the world in a vibrant spectrum of joy and simplicity.

The boys, on the other hand, were either engaged in playful fights or kicking a football around with great enthusiasm. Their shouts and cheers filled the air as they chased the ball, their faces lit up with excitement. It was a scene of pure, unadulterated joy, a moment in time that seemed to belong to another world—a world from which I felt increasingly detached. They were always so full of energy, so alive in their movements, that it seemed like nothing else mattered to them at that moment.

I often found myself here, sitting alone and watching the world go by. It wasn't that I didn't want to join in; it was more that I didn't feel like I belonged. The tree was my sanctuary, a place where I could retreat into my thoughts and escape the chaos around me. As I watched my schoolmates, a part of me envied their carefree nature, their ability to immerse themselves in the moment without a second thought. Their laughter, their cries of triumph and defeat, it all seemed so distant and unreachable, like a dream that I could observe but never partake in.

The shadows under the tree were comforting, a stark contrast to the glaring sunlit playground. The leaves rustled gently in the breeze, whispering secrets of a world that moved too fast for me to keep up. I traced patterns in the dirt with a stick, lost in the rhythmic motion. It was calming, this repetitive action, and it allowed my mind to wander freely. The solitude was both a comfort and a curse; it gave me space to think but also highlighted my isolation.

## *The Weight of Loneliness*

As I sat there, lost in my thoughts, I couldn't help but feel a deep sense of longing and sadness. Everyone around me seemed so lucky. They had parents who cared for them, who dropped them off at school with smiles and hugs, who attended school events and cheered them on. My parents, on the other hand, were always fighting. Their arguments seemed to have no end, each one more intense than the last. They fought with everyone, without any reason, and it always seemed so pointless.

I often wondered why they even got married if all they did was argue. The constant fighting had created a chasm between us, a void that I didn't know how to fill. It made me feel like an outsider, not just at school but in my own home as well. The few times they did come to school, their presence was marked by stress and awkward silences. It was embarrassing, and it made me wish I could just disappear.

Sometimes, I imagined what it would be like to have a different life—a life where my parents were happy, where I had friends to play with, and where I felt like I belonged. But those were just dreams, fleeting thoughts that vanished as quickly as they came. Reality was different, and I had learned to live with it, even if it meant sitting alone under a tree, watching the world go by.

Their fights echoed in my mind, a never-ending loop of raised voices and harsh words. I would often lie in bed, staring at the ceiling, trying to shut out the noise. My parent's arguments were like a storm that never ended, leaving a trail of destruction in its wake. It was exhausting, trying to navigate the aftermath of their conflicts while keeping up with school and everything else.

Seeing my classmates with their happy families only deepened my sense of isolation. Their lives seemed perfect, filled with love and support, while mine felt like a constant struggle. It wasn't just the arguments that bothered me; it was the silence that followed. The cold, uncomfortable silence that settled in after their fights, making the house feel even more empty and hostile.

I often sought refuge in my room, burying myself in books or schoolwork. It was my way of escaping, of creating a world where I had some semblance of control. But no matter how hard I tried, the reality of my situation always found a way to creep back in, reminding me of the life I couldn't escape.

### *A Moment of Confrontation*

Lost in my thoughts, I didn't notice Miss Dangre approaching. She was my class teacher, a kind woman who always seemed to have a smile on her face. Her presence was comforting, a stark contrast to the turmoil I felt inside. As she came closer, I snapped out of my reverie and looked up, trying to muster a smile.

"Tathastu, why are you sitting here all alone?" she asked gently. "Why don't you go and play with the other kids?"

Her words were well-meaning, but they felt like a punch to the gut. I didn't want to explain why I preferred my own company, why the thought of joining the others filled me with dread. Instead, I just shrugged and looked away, hoping she would leave me alone.

Miss Dangre didn't press further. She simply nodded and gave me a reassuring pat on the shoulder before walking away. But her words lingered, making me feel even more isolated. The truth was, I didn't know how to connect with the others. I didn't know how to break free from the shadows of my thoughts and join the world around me.

Feeling overwhelmed, I stood up and walked away, heading back to my classroom. It was empty, the silence a stark contrast to the lively playground. I sat down at my desk and buried my head in my arms, wishing for an escape from the loneliness that seemed to envelop me.

The classroom was my refuge, a place where I could hide from the world and lose myself in my studies. It wasn't much, but it was all I had. As I sat there, the sound of the playground faded into the background, replaced by the hum of the ceiling fan and the ticking of the clock. Another day in my boring life, another day of feeling like an outsider in my own world.

## Chapter - 2
# Interests and Observations

***Discovering Dexter's Laboratory***

I sat cross-legged on the floor, eyes glued to the old television set that flickered with the bright colors of my favorite cartoon, "Dexter's Laboratory." Dexter, the boy genius with a hidden lab, always fascinated me. His inventions, his experiments, and his boundless curiosity made the show more than just entertainment—it was an escape into a world of endless possibilities. One episode in particular caught my attention that day. Dexter was talking about hacks to make the brain more active. As I watched, my interest piqued, and a spark ignited within me.

Dexter spoke about various techniques, methods that could supposedly enhance brain function. Simple tricks like using certain sounds to improve concentration, the benefits of reading books to increase knowledge and cognitive abilities, and even the importance of plants in improving mental health. The episode was like a goldmine of information, and I found myself scribbling notes frantically, trying to capture every detail.

As the episode ended, I felt an unusual sense of excitement. For the first time in a long while, I felt genuinely engaged in something. I wanted to learn more, to dive deeper into these hacks and see if they really worked. Dexter's world was fictional, but the ideas he presented seemed real enough to explore.

## *Diving into Books*

Determined to understand more, I started visiting the school library. It was a small, quiet place, with shelves lined with books that seemed to contain endless knowledge. I began with the basics—books on the human brain, psychology, and simple hacks to improve mental function. Each page I turned revealed something new, something fascinating. I learned about the different parts of the brain, how they functioned, and how certain activities could stimulate brain activity.

Reading became my refuge. It was a way to escape the chaos at home, to immerse myself in a world where I had control. I would lose myself in the books, forgetting for a while the constant fights between my parents, the feelings of loneliness, and the sense of being an outsider. The more I read, the more I wanted to learn. Each book was a doorway to new knowledge, new insights that fueled my growing interest in understanding the brain and how it worked.

I started implementing some of the hacks I read about. Simple things like doing puzzles to enhance problem-solving skills, practicing mindfulness to improve concentration, and even trying to maintain a healthier diet to support brain function. It was a slow process, but I could feel the difference. My mind felt sharper, more active. For the first time, I felt a sense of purpose, a goal to strive towards.

## Chapter - 2
# Interests and Observations

### *Discovering Dexter's Laboratory*

I sat cross-legged on the floor, eyes glued to the old television set that flickered with the bright colors of my favorite cartoon, "Dexter's Laboratory." Dexter, the boy genius with a hidden lab, always fascinated me. His inventions, his experiments, and his boundless curiosity made the show more than just entertainment—it was an escape into a world of endless possibilities. One episode in particular caught my attention that day. Dexter was talking about hacks to make the brain more active. As I watched, my interest piqued, and a spark ignited within me.

Dexter spoke about various techniques, methods that could supposedly enhance brain function. Simple tricks like using certain sounds to improve concentration, the benefits of reading books to increase knowledge and cognitive abilities, and even the importance of plants in improving mental health. The episode was like a goldmine of information, and I found myself scribbling notes frantically, trying to capture every detail.

As the episode ended, I felt an unusual sense of excitement. For the first time in a long while, I felt genuinely engaged in something. I wanted to learn more, to dive deeper into these hacks and see if they really worked. Dexter's world was fictional, but the ideas he presented seemed real enough to explore.

### *Diving into Books*

Determined to understand more, I started visiting the school library. It was a small, quiet place, with shelves lined with books that seemed to contain endless knowledge. I began with the basics—books on the human brain, psychology, and simple hacks to improve mental function. Each page I turned revealed something new, something fascinating. I learned about the different parts of the brain, how they functioned, and how certain activities could stimulate brain activity.

Reading became my refuge. It was a way to escape the chaos at home, to immerse myself in a world where I had control. I would lose myself in the books, forgetting for a while the constant fights between my parents, the feelings of loneliness, and the sense of being an outsider. The more I read, the more I wanted to learn. Each book was a doorway to new knowledge, new insights that fueled my growing interest in understanding the brain and how it worked.

I started implementing some of the hacks I read about. Simple things like doing puzzles to enhance problem-solving skills, practicing mindfulness to improve concentration, and even trying to maintain a healthier diet to support brain function. It was a slow process, but I could feel the difference. My mind felt sharper, more active. For the first time, I felt a sense of purpose, a goal to strive towards.

## *The Joy of Nurturing Plants*

Alongside my newfound interest in the brain, I discovered another passion—gardening. It started with a small plant my mother had placed on the windowsill. I began taking care of it, watering it daily, and watching it grow. There was something incredibly soothing about nurturing a living thing, watching it thrive under my care.

My collection of plants grew over time. Each new plant brought with it a sense of responsibility and joy. I would spend hours reading about different types of plants, their needs, and the best ways to care for them. The green corner of my room became my sanctuary, a place where I could find peace amidst the turmoil of my family life.

Taking care of my plants became a daily ritual. Each morning, I would check on them, ensuring they had enough water and sunlight. The routine brought a sense of stability to my life, a break from the unpredictability of my parent's arguments. My plants became my companion, silent but constant in their presence.

## *The Gift of Music*

On my thirteenth birthday, amidst the usual chaos of our household, my father surprised me with a gift—a flute. It was a simple instrument, but to me, it was a treasure. My father wasn't one for grand gestures, so this gift meant a lot. It was a moment of connection, a rare glimpse of his love amidst the usual distance.

I started learning to play the flute, finding solace in the gentle notes that filled the air. At first, it was just a series of clumsy attempts, but with practice, I started to improve.

The music became another escape, a way to express myself when words failed. I would play for hours, losing myself in the melodies, letting the music wash over me and carry me away from the troubles at home.

Playing the flute also became a way to drown out the noise of my parent's fights. Whenever their arguments became too much to bear, I would retreat to my room and play, letting the music block out the shouting. It was a small comfort, but it helped me cope with the tension and stress that had become a constant part of my life.

### *The Reality of Family Life*

Despite finding solace in my interests, the reality of my family life was always there, a shadow that loomed over everything. My parent's arguments seemed to intensify with each passing day. They fought over everything and nothing, their voices rising in anger over the smallest of issues. The tightness in our home was palpable, a heavy weight that pressed down on all of us.

We lived in a small, cramped apartment with only two bedrooms. My sister, who was three years older than me, and I shared one room, while our parents had the other.

There was little privacy, and the constant proximity only seemed to fuel the arguments. My sister tried to act as a buffer, but there was only so much she could do.

Nights were the hardest. The walls of our room seemed to close in on me, amplifying every word of their fights. I would lie awake, staring at the ceiling, wishing for silence. My sister, who slept beside me, often reached out to hold my hand, a silent gesture of comfort. We both knew there was nothing we could do to stop the fights, so we just endured them, finding solace in each other's presence.

### *Finding Moments of Peace*

Amidst the chaos, there were moments of peace—brief, fleeting, but precious. Early mornings, before the world woke up, became my sanctuary. I would wake up before everyone else, slipping out of bed quietly to avoid waking my sister. The house was still and silent, a stark contrast to the usual noise and tightness.

I would sit by the window, flute in hand, and play softly. The gentle notes filled the quiet air, a melody that brought a sense of calm. In those moments, I felt connected to something bigger, something beyond the walls of our small apartment. The music was a reminder that there was beauty in the world, even amidst the chaos.

My plants, too, provided a source of comfort. Their steady growth, the way they thrived under my care, was a reminder that life could flourish even in difficult circumstances. I took pride in their health, in the small garden I had created in my corner of the room. It was a symbol of hope, a testament to my ability to nurture and care.

### *A Glimmer of Hope*

Despite the constant fights and tightness, there were moments when I saw a glimmer of hope. My parents, though often at odds, had their moments of peace. They would sometimes sit together in silence, a rare truce in their ongoing battle. In those moments, I dared to hope that things could get better.

My sister and I found ways to cope, to create pockets of joy amidst the chaos. We would share stories, laugh over silly things, and support each other through the tough times. She was my confidante, my anchor in the storm. Her presence made the fights more bearable, the silence less lonely.

# Chapter - 3
# First Seizure

### *The Trip to Nagpur*

It was a sudden decision, one that caught me off guard. My father had received a call early in the morning, and the moment he hung up, I could see the stress in his face. His usually stern expression was replaced with one of worry, and his voice was uncharacteristically soft as he spoke to my mother. I could tell something was wrong, but I didn't ask any questions. I just watched as they hurriedly packed our bags and made arrangements for our trip to Nagpur, my dad's birthplace.

Nagpur was a small town, and though I had heard about it countless times from my father, we rarely visited. The last time we went there, I was too young to remember much. As we drove through the narrow, winding roads, I noticed how different it was from the city. The houses were smaller, the streets less crowded, and there was a sense of calm that was absent in our daily lives. Despite the serene surroundings, my parents seemed tense. They exchanged worried glances and spoke in hushed tones, their anxiety palpable.

The drive felt longer than usual, probably because of the heavy atmosphere in the car. My father gripped the steering wheel tightly, his knuckles white from the pressure. My mother sat beside him, her hands clenched in her lap, her eyes darting nervously between my father and the road ahead. They spoke in whispers, their words too quiet for me to hear, but the tension was evident.

I sat in the backseat with my sister, who tried to distract me with stories and games. She told me about her friends, about school, and even made up silly tales to make me laugh. But my mind kept wandering back to my parents and the stress that filled the car. I wondered what could be so urgent that we had to leave so suddenly. My sister seemed to sense my unease and gave me a reassuring smile, but it did little to ease my anxiety.

As we approached Nagpur, the scenery changed. The bustling cityscape gave way to open fields and small clusters of houses. The air felt different too—cleaner, fresher. The sight of the familiar landmarks brought back faint memories of my previous visits, but they were overshadowed by the current situation.

When we finally arrived, the air was heavy with grief. My father's relatives were gathered outside the house, their faces somber. My father spoke to a few of them, his voice breaking as he relayed the news to us—my dadi, his mother, had passed away. She was old, and her health had been declining for years, but the news still hit my father hard. I watched as he struggled to keep his emotions in check, his eyes brimming with tears.

### *A Disconnect from Grief*

Despite the somber atmosphere, I felt strangely detached. I had never been close to my dadi, and her death didn't evoke the emotions I thought it should. As everyone around me mourned, I felt an unsettling numbness. I could see the pain in my father's eyes, the way he held my mother tightly, seeking comfort. My sister cried softly, her tears mingling with the quiet whispers of condolence that filled the room. But I felt nothing.

I tried to understand why I was so disconnected. Was it because I hadn't known her well? Or was it something deeper, something wrong with me? The people around me were absorbed in their grief, their sobs and wails a testament to the loss they felt. I watched as they clung to each other, seeking solace in shared pain. But for me, it was as if I were observing a scene from a distance, detached and unaffected.

As the day wore on, I wandered through the house, trying to make sense of my feelings. The walls were lined with photographs, each one telling a story of happier times. I saw pictures of my father as a young boy, smiling with my dadi. There were family gatherings, celebrations, and moments frozen in time. I stared at the photos, searching for a connection, a spark of emotion, but found none.

The house itself felt foreign. It was filled with people I barely knew, relatives who came up to me with tearful eyes and sympathetic smiles. They tried to engage me in conversation, to share their memories of my dadi, but their words washed over me like a distant echo. I nodded politely, murmured responses, but inside, I felt empty.

### *The Collapse*

The next thing I knew, darkness enveloped me. I felt weightless, like I was floating in a void. Time lost all meaning, and the world around me faded away. When I finally opened my eyes, I was no longer in my dadi's house. Instead, I found myself in a stark, sterile room, surrounded by the soft hum of machines.

I blinked, trying to make sense of my surroundings. The ceiling was white, with harsh fluorescent lights casting a cold glow. I could hear the steady beeping of monitors and the faint sound of footsteps outside the door. Confused and disoriented, I looked down and saw wires and tubes connected to my body, their ends attached to various machines that beeped and whirred around me.

I glanced at the clock on the wall—it was 12:16 at night. The realization that I was in a hospital hit me like a punch to the gut. Panic began to rise within me, my heart racing as I tried to remember how I had ended up here.

### *A Mother's Tears*

As I struggled to piece together what had happened, I noticed my mother sitting beside me. Her face was pale, her eyes red and swollen from crying. She looked up as I stirred, her expression a mix of relief and worry. She reached out and gently held my hand, her grip firm yet trembling.

"Tathastu, thank God you're awake," she whispered, her voice breaking. Tears streamed down her cheeks, and she wiped them away with the back of her hand. "You scared us so much."

My mind was a whirlwind of questions. Why was I here? What had happened to me? But before I could speak, my sister appeared at my other side. She looked just as shaken, her usual calm demeanor replaced with concern.

"You'll be fine," she said softly, squeezing my hand. Her presence was comforting, a beacon of stability in the midst of my confusion.

My mother's tears flowed freely now, her sobs breaking the silence of the room. "When we found you, you were unresponsive. We thought we had lost you," she said, her voice trembling. "The doctors didn't know if you would wake up."

I squeezed her hand weakly, trying to offer some comfort. "I'm here, Mom. I'm okay," I whispered, though I wasn't entirely sure if I believed it myself.

### *The Doctor's Explanation*

A few moments later, the door opened, and a doctor walked in. He was an older man with a kind face, his expression one of professional concern. He checked the monitors and my vital signs before turning to my mother.

"Mr. Tathastu, your son has experienced a very rare type of seizure," he began, his voice calm and measured. "Typically, during a seizure, the brain undergoes a sort of reset. However, in Tathastu's case, his brain activity ceased entirely for an extended period. It was as if he were in a state of clinical death. No brain activity, no heartbeat, nothing. For 166 minutes, all his organs had shut down, including his heart and brain."

My mother gasped, her grip on my hand tightening. The doctor continued, "We were certain we had lost him. But then, inexplicably, his brain activity resumed, and his heart started beating again. This is the first time I've encountered such a case. It's truly unbelievable."

The doctor's words were almost too much to take in. I felt a mix of disbelief and fear. How could I have been dead for nearly three hours and then just come back? It didn't make sense. The doctor's explanation was clinical, detached, but the gravity of his words hit me hard.

## *Processing the Unbelievable*

I listened to the doctor's words, trying to comprehend what he was saying. The idea that I had been essentially dead for 166 minutes was overwhelming. I felt a mixture of fear, confusion, and a strange sense of detachment, as if he were talking about someone else entirely.

The doctor turned to me, his eyes filled with a mixture of curiosity and compassion. "Tathastu, you've experienced something very rare and very profound. We're going to run some more tests to understand what happened and how we can prevent it from happening again."

My mother nodded, her face a mask of worry and relief. She looked at me, her eyes filled with unspoken fears and questions. "We'll do whatever it takes to keep you safe," she whispered, her voice trembling with emotion.

My sister stayed by my side, her presence a comforting constant amidst the confusion. She held my hand and reassured me, her voice steady even as her eyes betrayed her worry. "We'll get through this, Tathastu. You're strong, and we'll find a way to make sure this doesn't happen again."

## *The Aftermath*

The days that followed were a blur of tests, doctor visits, and long hours spent in the sterile confines of the hospital. The doctors were determined to understand the nature of my seizure and find ways to prevent another one. They spoke of brain waves, electrical activity, and neurological anomalies, terms that sounded foreign and frightening.

Through it all, my family remained by my side. My mother, despite her own fears, stayed strong, her presence a constant source of comfort. My sister, always supportive, helped me navigate the complexities of medical jargon and reassured me that we would find answers.

I tried to make sense of what had happened, but it was difficult. The idea that I had been clinically dead for nearly three hours was hard to grasp. I had no memory of that time, no sense of where I had been or what I had experienced. It was as if I had simply ceased to exist for those 166 minutes.

As I lay in the hospital bed, I replayed the events leading up to my collapse over and over in my mind. The drive to Nagpur, the tense atmosphere, my father's grief, and my own disconnect from the situation. It all seemed so surreal, like a bad dream that I couldn't wake up from.

The doctors conducted various tests, poking and prodding me with needles and attaching electrodes to my head. They monitored my brain activity, looking for any abnormalities that could explain what had happened. They scanned my brain, took blood samples, and asked me countless questions about my health and family history.

Each test felt invasive, a reminder of the fragility of my condition. I hated the feeling of being a lab rat, of having my every move scrutinized and analyzed. But I knew it was necessary. The doctors were doing their best to find answers, and I had to trust that they would.

My mother and sister took turns staying with me, never leaving me alone for too long. Their presence was a comfort, a reminder that I wasn't facing this alone. My father, though visibly shaken, tried to put on a brave face. He would sit by my bed, holding my hand and telling me stories of his own childhood, trying to distract me from the fear and uncertainty.

The hospital room became my world, a small bubble of safety amidst the chaos. The nurses were kind, always checking in on me and making sure I was comfortable. They brought me meals, adjusted my bed, and even tried to cheer me up with small talk and jokes.

Despite their efforts, I couldn't shake the feeling of unease. The knowledge that I had been so close to death lingered in the back of my mind, a constant reminder of my own mortality. I tried to stay positive, to focus on the fact that I had survived, but it was hard. The fear of another seizure, another brush with death, hung over me like a dark cloud.

As the days passed, the doctors began to piece together a picture of what had happened. They explained that my seizure had caused a temporary shutdown of my brain and other vital organs. It was a rare occurrence, one that they didn't fully understand, but they were determined to find a way to prevent it from happening again.

They prescribed medication to help stabilize my brain activity and reduce the risk of another seizure. They also recommended regular check-ups and monitoring to keep an eye on my condition. It was a lot to take in, but I knew it was necessary.

My family and I left the hospital with a sense of cautious optimism. The road ahead was uncertain, but we were determined to face it together. The first seizure had been a wake-up call, a reminder of the fragility of life and the importance of cherishing every moment.

## Chapter - 4
# Weird Feelings and Incidents Post-Seizure

### *Returning Home*

After several days in the hospital, I was finally discharged. The doctors had done all they could to understand my condition and stabilize it with medication. They gave us a list of prescriptions and instructions, and a solemn warning to monitor my condition closely. As we left the hospital, I felt a mixture of relief and trepidation. The sterile, clinical environment was behind me, but the uncertainty of my health loomed large.

The journey back home felt surreal. My mother kept glancing at me from the front seat, her eyes filled with worry and relief. My father focused on the road, his grip on the steering wheel tighter than usual. My sister sat next to me, her presence a silent comfort. As we drove through the familiar streets, I tried to shake off the unease that clung to me.

When we finally arrived, our house felt different. It was the same small, cramped apartment we had left, but it seemed heavier somehow, weighed down by the recent events. My parents tried to act normally, but the traction was palpable. They were extra cautious, constantly asking if I felt okay, if I needed anything.

My room, once a place of refuge, now felt unfamiliar. The bed, the books, the plants—they were all the same, yet everything felt different. It was as if a veil had been lifted, revealing the fragile nature of my existence. I sat on my bed, looking around, trying to reconnect with the space that had always been my sanctuary.

That night, as I lay in bed, I found it difficult to sleep. The events of the past few days played over and over in my mind. The hospital, the doctors, the beeping machines—it all felt like a nightmare. I could still hear the doctor's words echoing in my head: "For 166 minutes, all his organs had shut down, including his heart and brain." The gravity of those words was overwhelming. I had been clinically dead, yet here I was, alive and confused.

The next morning, my mother woke me up early to take my medication. The pills were supposed to stabilize my brain activity and prevent another seizure, but they came with their own set of challenges. I quickly realized that these medications had side effects. My brain felt slow, like it was wading through molasses. Tasks that once felt easy now required extra effort. My thoughts were sluggish, and concentrating became a struggle.

Despite this, I tried to resume my normal routine. I went back to school, hoping to find solace in familiar surroundings. The first day back was overwhelming. My classmates looked at me with curiosity and concern, their whispers following me down the hallways. I forced a smile, pretending that everything was fine, but inside, I felt anything but normal.

During recess, I found my usual spot under the tree. The playground was alive with activity, just as it had always been. The girls played their games, and the boys chased the football with their usual enthusiasm. I sat in the shade, watching them, trying to recapture the sense of peace I once found there.

## *The Effects of Medication*

The medication made everything feel dull. Colors seemed less vibrant, sounds were muffled, and my thoughts moved at a sluggish pace. It was like living in a fog, where everything was muted and distant. I struggled to keep up with my schoolwork, often finding myself staring blankly at the pages of my textbooks, unable to focus.

The teachers noticed the change in me. Miss Dangre, in particular, was concerned. She pulled me aside one day after class, her eyes filled with worry. "Tathastu, are you feeling okay? You've been very quiet lately," she said gently.

I nodded, forcing a smile. "I'm fine, Miss Dangre. Just a bit tired, that's all."

She didn't seem convinced but didn't press further. "If you need anything, or if you want to talk, I'm here for you," she offered.

I appreciated her concern, but I didn't know how to explain what I was going through. How could I articulate the feeling of being trapped in a slow-motion world, where everything moved at a different pace than my mind? How could I describe the constant haze that clouded my thoughts?

## *A Strange Sensation*

As I sat there, I felt a strange sensation. It was subtle at first, a faint whisper at the edge of my consciousness. I ignored it, attributing it to the side effects of the medication. But the feeling grew stronger, more insistent. It felt as if the tree was talking to me. I shook my head, trying to clear my thoughts, but the sensation persisted.

I looked around, half-expecting to see someone playing a prank, but the playground was as it always was. The tree, with its wide branches and rustling leaves, seemed to be whispering secrets to me. I felt a chill run down my spine. This wasn't normal. Trees don't talk. But the feeling was so strong, so real, that I couldn't ignore it.

Panic set in, and I quickly got up and headed back to my classroom. My heart raced, and my mind was a whirl of confusion and fear. What was happening to me? Was this a side effect of the medication, or was it something else? I tried to focus on my studies, but my thoughts kept drifting back to the tree and the strange sensation.

Throughout the day, the feeling lingered. It was as if the tree had left an imprint on my mind, a reminder of something beyond my understanding. I couldn't shake the sensation, couldn't forget the whispering leaves. It haunted me, a constant background noise that I couldn't tune out.

I started to question my sanity. Was I losing my mind? The idea terrified me. I had always been a logical person, someone who sought explanations and understood the world through reason. But this—this was beyond reason. It was something inexplicable, something that defied logic.

That night, I lay in bed, staring at the ceiling. The room was dark and silent, but my mind was a whirlwind of thoughts. I replayed the events of the day, the whispering tree, the sensation that had felt so real. I tried to make sense of it, but there were no answers. Just more questions, more confusion.

### *Reflections on the Seizure*
Next day in the school.

As I sat in class, pretending to pay attention to the lessons, my mind wandered to the seizure. The doctor's words echoed in my mind: "For 166 minutes, all his organs had shut down, including his heart and brain." The gravity of those words was still hard to grasp. I had been clinically dead, yet here I was, alive and confused.

I wondered what had happened during those 166 minutes. Where had I been? What had I experienced? There were no memories, no dreams, just a blank void. It was as if a part of my life had been erased. I thought about the doctor's explanation, about the brain reset that usually occurs during a seizure. But in my case, it was different. My brain activity had ceased entirely, and then, miraculously, it had resumed.

These thoughts consumed me, making it hard to focus on anything else. I felt like I was living in a strange dream, disconnected from reality. The more I thought about it, the more questions I had. Why had this happened to me? Was there something abnormal about my brain? And most importantly, would it happen again?

The seizure had left a mark on me, a scar that was invisible but deeply felt. It was a constant reminder of my fragility, of the thin line between life and death. I tried to push these thoughts away, to focus on the present, but they always crept back in, uninvited and persistent.

My classmates noticed the change in me. They whispered among themselves, casting curious glances in my direction. I could feel their eyes on me, could hear the murmurs of speculation. It was unsettling, this sudden attention. I had always preferred to blend into the background, to be unnoticed. But now, I was the center of their curiosity, and it made me uncomfortable.

### *Seeking Answers*

After school, I decided to visit the bookstore. I needed answers, and books had always been a reliable source of information for me. The bookstore was a small, cozy place with shelves lined with books on every subject imaginable. I browsed the shelves, looking for anything related to the brain and seizures.

I found a book titled "All About the Brain and Seizures" and eagerly flipped through its pages. The book was filled with scientific explanations, case studies, and theories about how the brain works and what happens during a seizure. I read about different types of seizures, their causes, and the treatments available. But the more I read, the more I realized that my experience didn't fit into any of the categories described in the book.

The book talked about electrical disturbances in the brain, the role of neurotransmitters, and the various factors that could trigger a seizure. It mentioned that in most cases, the brain undergoes a reset during a seizure, temporarily disrupting normal function but then returning to baseline activity. But there was nothing about a brain that completely shuts down for an extended period and then miraculously starts working again.

I felt a growing sense of frustration. The book provided no answers to my unique situation. It was as if what had happened to me was unprecedented, something that hadn't been documented before. The more I read, the more questions I had. If the doctors didn't understand my condition and the books didn't provide any insight, where could I turn for answers?

The bookstore was usually a place of solace for me, a haven where I could lose myself in the pages of a good book. But today, it felt different. The familiar shelves, the quiet atmosphere, the smell of paper and ink—they did little to soothe my troubled mind. I felt restless, unsettled, as if the answers I sought were just out of reach.

I continued to browse the shelves, picking up books on neurology, psychology, and even alternative medicine. I was desperate for any information that could shed light on my condition. But the more I read, the more I realized that my experience was truly unique. There were no documented cases of someone surviving such a prolonged shutdown of brain activity. It was as if I had ventured into uncharted territory.

## *Overwhelmed with Thoughts*

With so many thoughts swirling in my mind, I left the bookstore feeling more confused than ever. The streets outside were bustling with people going about their daily lives, oblivious to the turmoil within me. I walked slowly, lost in my thoughts, trying to make sense of everything.

As I walked, I thought about the strange sensation I had felt under the tree. It seemed so real, yet it was impossible. Trees don't talk. Was it a hallucination? A side effect of the medication? Or was it something else entirely? I couldn't shake the feeling that there was more to it, something beyond the realm of normal explanation.

By the time I reached home, it was late, and my family was already gathered for dinner. I joined them, trying to act normal, but my mind was elsewhere. The conversation around the table seemed distant, like background noise. I ate mechanically, my thoughts consumed by the events of the day.

After dinner, I retreated to my room, hoping for some peace and quiet. I lay on my bed, staring at the ceiling, replaying the day's events in my mind. The doctor's words, the sensation under the tree, the book that provided no answers—it all swirled together in a confusing mix.

I tried to distract myself by reading, but my mind kept drifting back to the seizure. The idea that I had been clinically dead for nearly three hours was hard to grasp. I had no memory of that time, no sense of where I had been or what I had experienced. It was as if a part of my life had been erased.

## *The Dream*

That night, I fell into a restless sleep, my mind still racing with thoughts and questions. I dreamed of a vast, green forest, filled with towering trees and vibrant plants. The colors were more vivid than anything I had ever seen, and the air was filled with a sense of tranquility and life.

In the dream, the plants seemed to be alive in a way that went beyond mere biology. They moved and swayed with a purpose, their leaves rustling in a symphony of whispers. As I walked through the forest, I felt a strange connection to the plants around me, as if they were trying to communicate with me.

The whispers grew louder, and I realized that the plants were indeed talking to me. Their voices were soft and melodic, blending together in a harmonious chorus. They spoke of things I didn't understand, of worlds beyond my own, of secrets hidden in the depths of nature. They seemed to be asking for my help, though I couldn't comprehend what they needed.

The dream felt incredibly real, more real than any dream I had ever had. I could feel the cool breeze on my skin, smell the fresh scent of the forest, and hear the rustling of the leaves. It was a sensory experience that went beyond mere imagination.

When I woke up in the morning, the dream lingered in my mind. It had felt so real, so vivid, that I couldn't dismiss it as just a product of my imagination. The feeling of connection to the plants, their voices asking for help—it all seemed to hint at something beyond my understanding.

I lay in bed, trying to make sense of the dream. It felt like a message, a glimpse into a world I couldn't fully grasp. I wondered if it was connected to the seizure, to the strange sensation I had felt under the tree. Was my brain trying to tell me something? Or was it just a coincidence?

As I got up and prepared for the day, the dream stayed with me. The sense of connection, the feeling of being called to help—it was all so overwhelming. I knew I couldn't ignore it, but I also didn't know what to do with it.

The day passed in a blur, my thoughts constantly drifting back to the dream. I went through the motions of my daily routine, but my mind was elsewhere. The strange feelings and incidents post-seizure had left me with more questions than answers, and I couldn't shake the feeling that there was something important I needed to understand.

# Chapter – 5
# Discovery of Jikoya

### *Restless Nights*

Since my first seizure and the strange dream that followed, sleep had become an elusive, almost mythical concept. Each night, as I lay down and closed my eyes, my mind refused to quiet down. Thoughts raced through my head, one after another, in a never-ending cascade of images and questions. The dream of the talking plants haunted me, replaying in vivid detail every time I closed my eyes. The colors, the sounds, the sense of connection—it all felt so real, so tangible, that I couldn't shake the feeling that it meant something important.

I tossed and turned, my body restless and my mind in turmoil. The bed, once a place of comfort and rest, now felt like a prison. The sheets tangled around me, the pillow offered no solace, and the ticking of the clock on the wall only served to remind me of the hours slipping away. Every night was the same: hours spent staring at the ceiling, my thoughts a chaotic jumble that refused to settle.

The lack of sleep took its toll. I felt constantly exhausted, my body heavy and my mind sluggish. The world around me seemed to move at a different pace, and I struggled to keep up. The once-familiar routines of my day felt alien, as if I were going through the motions without truly being present. My family noticed the change in me, their concerned looks and gentle questions only adding to my sense of frustration and helplessness.

The nights were the worst. Alone in the darkness, the quiet amplified my thoughts. I could hear every creak of the house, every distant sound from outside. It felt as if the world was closing in on me, the weight of my thoughts pressing down until I could barely breathe. I would lie awake for hours, my mind racing with questions and doubts. Why was this happening to me? What did the dream mean? Was it connected to the seizure, or was it something else entirely?

The dream itself was vivid, more real than any dream I had ever experienced. The plants in the dream seemed alive in a way that defied logic. They whispered to me, their voices soft and melodic, speaking of things I couldn't understand. It felt like they were trying to tell me something, something important. But no matter how hard I tried, I couldn't grasp the meaning of their words.

### *Daytime Distractions*

During the day, I tried to distract myself from the restless nights and the vivid dream that plagued me. School provided a temporary reprieve, a place where I could focus on something other than my own thoughts. But even there, the sense of disconnection lingered. I sat in class, pretending to pay attention, but my mind was always elsewhere. The words of the teachers became a distant drone, background noise to the thoughts that consumed me.

Recess was no better. I found my usual spot under the tree, hoping to find some semblance of peace. The playground was alive with activity, just as it had always been. The girls played their games, and the boys chased the football with their usual enthusiasm. But I couldn't focus on any of it. The whispering sensation I had felt under the tree before was stronger now, more insistent. It felt as if the tree and the plants around it were trying to communicate with me, their voices blending together in a soft, melodic chorus.

I shook my head, trying to clear my thoughts, but the sensation persisted. It was unsettling, this feeling of being connected to something beyond my understanding. The more I tried to ignore it, the stronger it became. It was as if the plants were calling out to me, asking for something I couldn't comprehend. The restlessness and confusion followed me everywhere, a constant presence that I couldn't escape.

In the classroom, I found it hard to concentrate on my studies. My thoughts kept drifting back to the dream, to the whispering plants and the sense of connection I couldn't explain. The textbooks in front of me seemed meaningless, the lessons irrelevant. I wanted answers, but I didn't know where to find them.

My teachers noticed the change in me. They saw my lack of focus, my distracted state. Miss Dangre, in particular, was concerned. She pulled me aside one day after class, her eyes filled with worry. "Tathastu, are you feeling okay? You've been acting so different," she said gently.

I nodded, forcing a smile. "I'm fine, Miss Dangre. Just normal headache, that's all."

She didn't seem convinced... "If you need anything, or if you want to talk, I'm here for you," she told

I appreciated her concern, but I didn't know how to explain what I was going through. How could I articulate the feeling of being trapped in a slow-motion world, where everything moved at a different pace than my mind? How could I describe the constant haze that clouded my thoughts?

## *Weird Thoughts and Talking Objects*

As the days passed, the strange sensations grew stronger. It wasn't just the plants anymore. Objects around me seemed to take on a life of their own. The books on my shelf, the toys in my room, even the furniture—they all seemed to whisper and hum with a faint, barely perceptible energy. It was as if the entire world had come alive, and I was the only one who could sense it.

I tried to dismiss these feelings as side effects of the medication, but the more I thought about it, the more I realized that this was something different. The whispers were too real, too persistent to be mere hallucinations. It felt as if the world around me was trying to communicate, to convey a message that I couldn't quite grasp.

The whispers filled my mind, making it difficult to focus on anything else. I found it hard to concentrate on my studies, my thoughts constantly drifting back to the strange sensations. The once-familiar environment of my home felt alien, as if I were living in a dream. The objects around me seemed to pulse with a hidden energy, their whispers blending together in a confusing symphony.

I became increasingly withdrawn, my family's concerns growing with each passing day. They tried to reach out, to understand what was happening, but I couldn't explain it to them. How could I put into words the feeling that everything around me was alive, that the very objects I interacted with were trying to speak to me? It was a concept that defied logic, that existed beyond the realm of normal understanding.

The nights were the worst. Alone in the darkness, the quiet amplified my thoughts. The whispers grew louder, more insistent, until I felt like I was going mad. I would lie awake for hours, listening to the murmurs of the objects around me, trying to make sense of their words. But they remained elusive, just beyond my grasp.

### *Seeking Understanding*

Determined to make sense of what was happening, I turned to books. Reading had always been a refuge for me, a way to escape the chaos of my thoughts. I spent hours in the library, poring over texts on dreams, the brain, and the nature of consciousness. I searched for anything that could explain the strange sensations I was experiencing, hoping to find some clue, some answer that would make sense of it all.

I read about the different stages of sleep, the role of dreams, and the ways in which the brain processes information. I learned about the subconscious mind, about how it can influence our perceptions and experiences. But none of it seemed to apply to my situation. The books provided theories and explanations, but they didn't account for the vivid dream of the talking plants or the persistent whispers of the objects around me.

Frustration mounted as my search for answers yielded nothing. I felt as if I were chasing shadows, each clue leading to another dead end. The more I read, the more questions I had. Was this all in my mind? A side effect of the seizure or the medication? Or was there something more, something beyond the realm of conventional understanding?

The library, usually a place of solace, became a source of frustration. I scoured the shelves, seeking out books on neurology, psychology, and even paranormal phenomena. I was desperate for any information that could shed light on my condition. But the more I read, the more I realized that my experience was truly unique. There were no documented cases of someone surviving such a prolonged shutdown of brain activity and experiencing the sensations I was.

### *The Search for Dream Substances*

In my quest for understanding, I came across references to substances that could enhance dream recall. These substances, often derived from plants or synthesized in laboratories, were said to have the ability to unlock the subconscious mind, allowing individuals to remember their dreams in vivid detail. The idea intrigued me. If I could recall my dreams more clearly, perhaps I could make sense of the vivid dream of the talking plants and the strange sensations that followed.

I delved deeper into the topic, reading everything I could find about these substances. Some were ancient, used in traditional rituals and practices to induce lucid dreaming and heightened states of awareness. Others were modern creations, developed by scientists exploring the boundaries of human consciousness. The more I read, the more fascinated I became. These substances seemed to hold the key to understanding my experiences, to unlocking the mysteries that plagued my mind.

But as I continued my research, I discovered that many of these substances were banned. Their effects on the brain were poorly understood, and their use was often associated with significant risks. Despite the warnings, I couldn't shake the feeling that this was the path I needed to follow. The desire to understand my dreams, to make sense of the whispers and sensations, drove me forward.

The more I learned, the more determined I became. I read about the history of these substances, about their use in various cultures and their purported effects. Some were said to induce vivid, lifelike dreams, while others were believed to enhance memory and recall. The possibilities seemed endless, and I was eager to explore them all.

But the road to understanding was fraught with obstacles. The substances I read about were often difficult to obtain, their use restricted or outright banned in many places. The risks associated with their use were also a significant concern. I read horror stories of people who had suffered severe side effects, their minds damaged by the very substances they had hoped would provide answers.

## *Exploring the Dark Web*

With the conventional avenues exhausted, I turned to the internet. The vast expanse of information available online seemed to hold endless possibilities. I watched countless YouTube videos, read forums and articles, and followed every lead I could find. One night, while browsing through videos, I stumbled upon a channel discussing the dark web. The creator talked about the hidden corners of the internet, where banned substances, including those for dream recall, could be found.

The concept of the dark web was both intriguing and intimidating. It was a place shrouded in mystery, where anonymity reigned and the boundaries of legality were often blurred. The more I learned about it, the more I felt a mix of curiosity and apprehension. The creator explained the steps to access the dark web, the precautions needed to stay safe, and the risks involved.

I watched the video multiple times, taking notes and trying to understand the process. The idea of venturing into the dark web was daunting, but it seemed like the only way to find the answers I sought. I needed to be cautious, to ensure that I didn't get in over my head. The thought of finding the substance that could help me recall my dreams was too tempting to ignore.

The video detailed the use of specialized software to access the dark web, the importance of maintaining anonymity, and the need for caution when navigating this hidden realm. I learned about the Tor browser, a tool designed to protect user identity by routing internet traffic through multiple servers, effectively masking the user's location. The idea was both fascinating and frightening, a digital labyrinth where one wrong turn could lead to danger.

As I prepared to take this step, a sense of determination settled over me. I was ready to explore the unknown, to delve into the hidden corners of the internet in search of answers. The dark web held the promise of understanding, of unlocking the secrets that had eluded me for so long. I knew the risks, but the desire to make sense of my experiences drove me forward.

Setting up the necessary software was a meticulous process. I followed the steps outlined in the video, ensuring that I downloaded everything from trusted sources. The installation of the Tor browser was straightforward, but the precautions I had to take were extensive.

Once I had everything set up, I took a deep breath and opened the Tor browser. The interface was simple, almost deceptively so. I navigated to the dark web directories, lists of websites hidden from the regular internet. These directories were like maps, guiding me through the shadowy landscape of the dark web.

## Chapter - 6
# Risk in the Dark Web

*Venturing into the Dark Web*

With everything installed and ready, I felt a mix of excitement and trepidation as I opened the Tor browser. The interface was simple, almost deceptively so. I navigated through the dark web directories, each click taking me deeper into a world that was both fascinating and frightening. The anonymity of the dark web was both its allure and its danger.

The initial steps were straightforward. I had followed the online tutorials meticulously, ensuring that I had the necessary protections in place. Using a virtual private network (VPN) added an extra layer of security, masking my location and encrypting my internet traffic. The Tor browser itself routed my connection through multiple servers around the world, making it nearly impossible for anyone to trace my activity back to me.

Despite these precautions, a sense of unease settled over me as I delved deeper into the dark web. The sites I encountered ranged from the mundane to the macabre. There were forums discussing everything from conspiracy theories to illegal activities, marketplaces selling counterfeit goods, and even hitman services. It was a shadowy underworld where morality was a distant memory, and anonymity allowed the darkest impulses to flourish.

One of the most unsettling discoveries was a live stream from a torture room. I quickly closed the tab, my heart pounding. The dark web was a place where the worst of humanity could thrive, hidden from the prying eyes of law enforcement. It was a sobering reminder of the risks I was taking by venturing here. The more I explored, the more I realized how careful I needed to be.

The further I delved, the more I encountered the disturbing realities of the dark web. The content ranged from illegal arms deals to explicit materials, each more horrifying than the last. It felt like I was walking through a digital minefield, where every click could lead to something more sinister.

Forums were filled with users discussing everything under the sun, from hacking techniques to illegal trades. Each thread was a deep dive into a world that was both foreign and frightening. I read about people exchanging information on how to obtain false identities, discussing ways to avoid law enforcement, and even plotting crimes.

Despite the horrors, I pressed on, determined to find the substances that could help me understand my dreams. The dark web was vast, and within its depths lay the answers I sought. I knew I had to tread carefully, but my curiosity and need for understanding pushed me forward.

### *Finding the Marketplaces*

I navigated to several marketplaces, digital bazaars where vendors sold everything from counterfeit documents to illegal drugs. Each marketplace had its own layout and user interface, but the principle was the same: anonymity and secrecy were paramount. These marketplaces were designed to resemble legitimate e-commerce sites, complete with user reviews, product descriptions, and seller ratings.

I browsed through the listings, my eyes scanning the descriptions and user reviews. It was a surreal experience, shopping for illegal substances as if I were on any other online store. I found several vendors selling Jikoya, the substance I had read about that could enhance dream recall. The listings described it as a powerful hallucinogen, capable of unlocking the deepest parts of the subconscious mind.

Most vendors required payment upfront, usually in cryptocurrency to maintain anonymity. The idea of sending money to a faceless stranger on the dark web was daunting. I read through user reviews, trying to gauge the reliability of each vendor. Some had glowing reviews, while others had warnings of scams and dangerous products.

Navigating these marketplaces was like walking through a minefield. Each click, each transaction carried inherent risks. There were horror stories of people being scammed, of receiving dangerous substances, or worse, being traced and prosecuted. But the desire to understand my dreams, to find some semblance of peace, pushed me forward.

I read through countless reviews, trying to determine which vendors were trustworthy. Some users shared their positive experiences, describing vivid dreams and enhanced recall. Others warned of counterfeit products and dangerous side effects. The reviews were a mixed bag, making it difficult to make a decision.

The marketplaces themselves were structured in a way that encouraged caution. Each listing came with a detailed description of the product, its effects, and potential risks. Vendors often included disclaimers, warning users to use the substances responsibly and at their own risk. Despite these warnings, the allure of Jikoya was too strong to ignore.

### *The Offline Deal*

As I continued my search, I found a vendor who offered a unique proposition. Unlike the others, he was willing to meet in person for the exchange. The location he suggested was just 20 kilometers away from my home, in a secluded area near a small bridge. It seemed risky, but the idea of a face-to-face transaction felt more secure than sending money into the void of the internet.

I initiated a chat with the vendor, using the encrypted messaging system provided by the marketplace. He responded quickly, his messages concise and to the point. He assured me that the Jikoya was of the highest quality and that the transaction would be quick and discreet. He asked for 100 Indian rupees, a surprisingly small amount for something so rare and powerful.

My curiosity outweighed my fear. I agreed to the deal and he provided the address, instructing me to meet him after dark. The whole setup seemed suspicious, but I was driven by a need to understand the strange experiences that had plagued me since my seizure. I prepared myself mentally for the encounter, knowing that I had to be cautious.

As the day of the meeting approached, my anxiety grew. I went over the plan repeatedly in my mind, trying to anticipate any possible dangers. The idea of meeting a stranger in a secluded area was nerve-wracking, but I couldn't shake the feeling that this was my chance to find answers. The days leading up to the meeting were filled with a tense anticipation, a mix of fear and excitement.

On the day of the meeting, I left home early, my heart pounding with a mix of fear and excitement. The route to the meeting spot was familiar, but each step felt heavy with the weight of my decision. I reviewed the vendor's instructions one last time, making sure I knew exactly where to go.

The bridge was an old, rusted structure, a relic from another era. It spanned a narrow river, its waters reflecting the dim light of the moon. The location was secluded, just as the vendor had promised, adding to the sense of danger that permeated the encounter.

### *The Meeting*

Sunday arrived, and I could barely focus on anything else. After school, I made my way to the meeting spot, my heart pounding with anticipation and fear. The sun had just set, casting long shadows over the deserted streets. The bridge was an old, rusted structure, a relic from another era. It spanned a narrow river, its waters reflecting the dim light of the moon.

I waited near the bridge, my eyes scanning the area for any sign of the vendor. The streets were eerily quiet, the only sound the occasional rustle of leaves in the wind. After what felt like an eternity, I saw a figure approaching. He was dressed in dark clothes, a mask covering his face. He walked with a purposeful stride, his eyes hidden behind dark sunglasses.

He gestured for me to follow him under the bridge, where the shadows were deepest. My heart raced as I complied, the sense of danger palpable. Once we were out of sight, he turned to me and asked for the money. I handed him the 100 rupees, my hands trembling slightly. He pocketed the money and pulled out a small packet, holding it up for me to see.

Just as I was about to reach for the packet, he pulled out a gun. The cold barrel pressed against my temple, and my heart nearly stopped. "Get in the car," he ordered, his voice a low growl. I glanced at the car parked nearby, the windows tinted dark. Panic surged through me, my mind racing for a way out.

At that moment, an ambulance roared down the street, its siren blaring. The noise startled the vendor, his grip on the gun faltering. The lights from the ambulance illuminated the scene, casting sharp shadows. Seizing the opportunity, I pushed away from him and ran. My feet pounded against the pavement, my breath coming in ragged gasps.

The vendor shouted after me, but the sound of the siren drowned out his words. I didn't look back, my only thought was to escape. The bridge and the surrounding streets blurred as I ran, my fear propelling me forward. I ducked into an alley, my heart hammering in my chest.

I hid behind a dumpster, my breath coming in short, panicked bursts. I waited, listening for any sign of pursuit. The minutes ticked by, each one feeling like an eternity. Finally, when I was sure the vendor wasn't following, I crept back to the bridge.

## *The Unexpected Escape*

The area was deserted, the only evidence of the encounter the dropped packet lying on the ground. I picked it up with trembling hands, my mind racing. I had the Jikoya, but at what cost? The fear and danger of the encounter weighed heavily on me, but the desire to understand my dreams pushed me forward.

I made my way home, the packet safely tucked away in my pocket. The journey back was a blur, my mind still reeling from the events of the night. Once home, I locked myself in my room, examining the packet with a mix of fear and anticipation. It was a small, unassuming package, but it held the promise of answers.

As I lay in bed that night, the events of the day played over and over in my mind. The dark web, the vendor, the gun—all of it felt like a surreal nightmare. But I had the Jikoya, the key to unlocking the mysteries that had haunted me since my seizure. The path ahead was uncertain and filled with risks, but I was ready to face it. The desire to understand, to find answers, drove me forward into the unknown.

For the next few days, I couldn't shake the sense of paranoia that gripped me. Every sound, every shadow seemed to hold a threat. I kept the Jikoya hidden, checking on it periodically to ensure it was still there. My family noticed my heightened anxiety, but I couldn't explain the source of my fear to them. How could I tell them about the dark web, the vendor, the gun? It was a secret I had to bear alone.

## *Alone at Home*

For the next few days, I was alone at home. My parents had to attend to some urgent family matters out of town, leaving my sister and me to fend for ourselves. My sister, busy with her own schoolwork and social life, was often out, leaving me with ample time to reflect on the recent events.

The solitude gave me a chance to process everything that had happened. The dark web, the vendor, the gun—it all felt like a surreal nightmare. But I had the Jikoya, the key to unlocking the mysteries that had haunted me since my seizure. The house, usually filled with the sounds of my family, was eerily quiet. The silence was both a comfort and a reminder of the dangers I had faced.

I spent my days in a haze, trying to act normal but constantly distracted by the events that had transpired. The packet of Jikoya was hidden in my room, a tangible reminder of the lengths I had gone to in search of answers. I couldn't shake the feeling of unease, the lingering fear that the vendor might come after me.

Each night, as I lay in bed, my mind raced with thoughts. The whispers from the objects around me seemed louder, more insistent. The vivid dream of the talking plants replayed in my mind, a constant reminder of why I had taken such risks. I knew that I couldn't ignore the call of the Jikoya. It was time to take the next step, to delve into the depths of my mind and uncover the truth behind my experiences.

The days alone gave me the chance to prepare mentally and physically for what was to come. I read more about Jikoya, understanding its effects and how to use it safely. I created a plan, knowing that the journey ahead would be fraught with risks and uncertainties. But I was ready, driven by the need to find answers and make sense of the chaos that had taken over my life.

The solitude also gave me a chance to reflect on the events that had led me to this point. The seizure, the strange sensations, the vivid dream—they were all pieces of a puzzle that I was determined to solve. The Jikoya held the promise of answers, the potential to unlock the secrets of my mind. I knew the risks, but the desire to understand, to find some semblance of peace, drove me forward.

As I held the packet in my hands, a sense of determination settled over me. I was ready to explore the unknown, to face the fears and dangers that lay ahead. The path was uncertain, but the desire to understand my dreams, to unlock the secrets of my mind, drove me forward. The journey into the depths of my consciousness was about to begin, and I was ready to face whatever came next.

## Chapter - 7
# Solution to Tackle Dark Matter

### *The Overwhelming Fear*

The packet of Jikoya sat on my desk, a small, unassuming envelope that held the promise of answers and the potential for danger. For days, I had stared at it, torn between the desire to understand my dreams and the fear of what might happen if I consumed it. The experiences I had gone through to obtain it were fresh in my mind, the encounter with the vendor and the near-death experience a stark reminder of the risks involved.

The fear was paralyzing. Every time I thought about taking the drug, my heart would race, and my palms would sweat. I had read countless accounts online about the effects of Jikoya, some describing profound, life-changing experiences, others warning of terrifying trips and dangerous side effects. The uncertainty of what I might experience weighed heavily on me.

I found myself pacing the room, the packet of Jikoya always within sight. The mere presence of it was enough to set my nerves on edge. Sometimes, I would pick it up, feeling its weight in my hands, contemplating the leap into the unknown. The stories I had read online played over and over in my mind, the vivid descriptions of both euphoric and harrowing experiences. The fear of losing control, of being trapped in a nightmarish hallucination, was a constant companion.

Yet, despite the fear, the strange sensations and whispers that had plagued me since my seizure grew stronger. It was as if the very world around me was urging me to take the next step, to uncover the truth hidden within my mind. The wooden objects in my room seemed to come alive, their whispers growing louder, more insistent. The desk, the bed frame, the bookshelf—they all seemed to speak to me, their voices blending into a chorus that I couldn't ignore.

### *The Decision*

The more I tried to ignore the whispers, the stronger they became. It felt as if I were caught in a web, each thread pulling me towards the inevitable moment when I would consume the Jikoya. The fear was still there, but it was overshadowed by the overwhelming need to understand the strange experiences that had taken over my life.

I spent hours researching online, reading everything I could find about how to consume Jikoya safely. Most accounts suggested crushing the substance into a fine powder, heating it, and inhaling the smoke. The process seemed simple enough, but the warnings about dosage and the potential for a bad trip were always present. The fear of the unknown, of losing control, made my heart race.

Each step of the process felt monumental. I watched videos and read forums, taking meticulous notes. Some users shared tips on how to prepare the substance, the best methods for inhalation, and how to minimize risks. I absorbed all this information, trying to prepare myself for what lay ahead. But no amount of preparation could fully quell the fear that gnawed at me.

Finally, one night, I couldn't take it anymore. The whispers were too loud, the urge too strong. I knew I had to take the next step, no matter the risk. I gathered the necessary materials: a spoon, a lighter, and a small piece of foil. My hands trembled as I prepared everything, the fear and anticipation making my heart pound in my chest.

The decision was not made lightly. I spent hours pacing, my mind a whirlwind of thoughts and doubts. The fear of the unknown was palpable, a tangible force that gripped my heart. But the desire to understand, to find answers, was stronger. I needed to know what the Jikoya would reveal, what secrets it would unlock within my mind.

### *Preparing the Jikoya*

With trembling hands, I opened the packet of Jikoya. Inside was a small amount of crystalline powder, its appearance unremarkable but its potential immense. I poured the powder onto a piece of foil, using the back of a spoon to crush it into an even finer consistency. The process was meticulous, each movement careful and deliberate. My heart raced as I worked, the reality of what I was about to do sinking in.

The powder sparkled under the dim light of my desk lamp, its tiny crystals catching the light and reflecting it back in a myriad of colors. I felt a strange mix of awe and fear as I crushed the crystals into a fine powder. Each press of the spoon felt like a step closer to the unknown, each movement deliberate and precise.

Once the powder was ready, I transferred it to a spoon, spreading it out evenly. The next step was to heat the spoon, allowing the Jikoya to vaporize so I could inhale the smoke. I held the lighter under the spoon, my hands shaking as the flame danced beneath it. The powder began to sizzle and melt, a thin wisp of smoke rising from the spoon.

I took a deep breath, trying to steady my nerves. The fear was overwhelming, but the desire to understand, to find answers, pushed me forward. I positioned myself over the spoon, ready to inhale the smoke. My heart pounded in my chest, the anticipation and fear almost unbearable.

### *Consuming the Jikoya*

With a final deep breath, I inhaled the smoke rising from the spoon. It was harsh and acrid, burning my throat and lungs. I coughed, my eyes watering, but I forced myself to take in as much as I could. The room seemed to spin, the edges of my vision blurring as the effects of the Jikoya began to take hold.

I stumbled back, my legs feeling weak and unsteady. The fear was still there, but it was accompanied by a strange sense of detachment, as if I were watching myself from a distance. The whispers around me grew louder, more insistent, their voices blending into a cacophony that filled my mind.

My heart raced, the fear and anticipation reaching a fever pitch. I tried to stand, but my legs wouldn't support me. It felt as if my body was shutting down, each muscle and organ going numb. Panic surged through me as I realized I couldn't move. I stumbled towards my bed, collapsing onto it as the world around me continued to spin.

I lay on the bed, staring up at the ceiling, my body feeling heavy and unresponsive. The whispers continued, a constant, insistent murmur that filled my mind. The fear was still there, but it was mingled with a strange sense of calm, as if I were on the brink of a profound revelation. The journey had begun, and there was no turning back.

---

## *Turn To Chapter 1: Right Hand Side (Page no. 144)*

---

## Chapter - 8
# Awakening Back to Normal Post Jikoya Effects

### *Regaining Consciousness*

The world around me was dark and silent. Slowly, I began to regain consciousness, feeling the soft surface beneath me. My senses were dulled, and my mind was foggy. As I opened my eyes, I found myself lying in my bed, the familiar surroundings of my room coming into focus. The events of the previous night, consuming Jikoya and the overwhelming sensations that followed, seemed like a distant, surreal memory.

I blinked several times, trying to clear the haze from my mind. The ceiling above me was just as I had left it, plain and unremarkable. I took a deep breath, feeling my chest rise and fall, and gradually the sensation of normalcy returned. My limbs felt heavy, but I managed to sit up and swing my legs over the side of the bed.

My head throbbed slightly, a dull ache that seemed to resonate with the disorientation I felt. I sat there for a moment, trying to gather my thoughts and make sense of the situation. Everything felt surreal, as if I were caught between two worlds – the familiar world of my bedroom and the strange, vivid realm of my hallucinations.

The details of the previous night began to come back to me in fragmented pieces. I remembered the intense visions, the feeling of my body shutting down, and the overwhelming sense of connection to something far beyond my understanding. It was both exhilarating and terrifying, and now, in the light of day, it seemed almost impossible to believe.

I glanced around my room, everything in its place, yet somehow different. It felt as if the entire world had shifted slightly, a subtle but undeniable change. The familiar objects – my desk, my bookshelf, the posters on the wall – all seemed to have a new significance, as if they were pieces of a puzzle I had yet to solve.

I noticed the small mirror on my bedside table and picked it up, examining my reflection. My eyes were clear, and there were no signs of the strange green glow I had seen before. I looked normal, but I couldn't shake the feeling that something within me had changed. There was a new depth to my gaze, a hint of the experiences I had just endured.

As I stared at my reflection, I couldn't help but wonder what lay beneath the surface. Had the Jikoya unlocked some hidden part of my consciousness? Or had it merely been a vivid hallucination, a trick of the mind? The questions swirled in my head, each one leading to more uncertainty.

### *Assessing the Situation*

As I sat on the edge of my bed, I tried to piece together what had happened. The vivid hallucinations and the intense feeling of my body shutting down were still fresh in my mind. I glanced around my room, everything in its place, yet somehow different. It felt as if the entire world had shifted slightly, a subtle but undeniable change.

I noticed the small mirror on my bedside table and picked it up, examining my reflection. My eyes were clear, and there were no signs of the strange green glow I had seen before. I looked normal, but I couldn't shake the feeling that something within me had changed.

I stood up slowly, testing my balance and strength. My legs felt wobbly, but I managed to walk to the bathroom. Splashing cold water on my face, I hoped it would help clear the lingering fog in my mind. The water felt refreshing, and I took a moment to stare at my reflection in the bathroom mirror, searching for any signs of the previous night's events.

As I returned to my room, I saw the packet of Jikoya lying on my desk. It looked harmless, almost mundane, but I knew the power it held. I picked it up, my hands trembling slightly, and carefully placed it back in the drawer where I had hidden it. The allure of the substance was strong, but so were the risks. I needed to be cautious.

The events of the night before replayed in my mind, each detail vivid and unsettling. The sensation of my body shutting down, the hallucinations that felt more real than reality itself, and the overwhelming sense of connection to another world – it was all too much to process. I felt a mixture of fear and curiosity, a deep desire to understand what had happened and why.

I glanced at the clock on my bedside table. It was early morning, the first light of dawn beginning to filter through the curtains. The house was still quiet, my family likely still asleep. I felt an overwhelming urge to talk to someone, to share what I had experienced, but I knew that no one would understand. How could they? I barely understood it myself.

I decided to take a walk outside, hoping that the fresh air would help clear my mind. I quietly slipped out of my room and made my way to the front door, careful not to wake anyone. The cool morning air greeted me as I stepped outside, a welcome contrast to the stifling atmosphere of my room.

As I walked through the quiet streets of my neighborhood, I tried to make sense of my thoughts. The hallucinations had felt incredibly real, and I couldn't dismiss them as mere illusions. The experience had left me with more questions than answers. What had I seen? Was there a deeper meaning behind those visions? And why did it feel so connected to my previous seizures?

### *The Aftermath*

I continued walking, lost in thought. The streets were empty, the world still waking up. I felt a strange sense of detachment, as if I were observing everything from a distance. The familiar surroundings of my neighborhood seemed foreign, like a dreamscape I couldn't quite place.

I walked to a nearby park, finding a quiet bench to sit on. The morning light filtered through the trees, casting dappled shadows on the ground. I took a deep breath, letting the tranquility of the moment wash over me. The questions and uncertainties still lingered, but for now, I allowed myself to simply be.

I watched as the park slowly came to life. Birds chirped in the trees, their songs filling the air. A few early risers jogged along the paths, their footsteps a rhythmic cadence. The world seemed to move on, indifferent to the turmoil in my mind. I envied their simplicity, their ability to go about their lives without the weight of unanswerable questions.

As I sat there, I couldn't help but replay the events of the previous night in my mind. The vivid hallucinations, the intense sensations, the overwhelming sense of connection – it all seemed so real, yet so impossible. I wondered if anyone else had experienced something similar. Was there a way to understand what had happened to me?

I decided to distract myself by focusing on my daily routine. I went back to home. I got dressed and headed to the kitchen, where the familiar smells of breakfast greeted me. My family was already up, my sister chatting with my mom while my dad read the newspaper. They looked up as I entered, their faces reflecting a mix of concern and relief.

"Morning, Tathastu," my mom said gently. "How are you feeling?"

I forced a smile, trying to appear normal. "I'm okay, Mom. Just a bit tired."

My sister gave me a sympathetic look. "You seemed out of its last night. Are you sure you're alright?"

I nodded, not wanting to worry them. "Yeah, just had a weird dream, I guess."

They accepted my explanation, and we settled into our usual breakfast routine. The familiar sounds and smells helped ground me, but the questions and uncertainties still lingered in the back of my mind.

As we ate, I tried to engage in the conversation, but my mind kept drifting back to the events of the previous night. I felt a strange disconnection from my family, as if I were living in a different reality. They talked about mundane things – school, work, plans for the weekend – while I struggled to come to terms with an experience that defied explanation.

After breakfast, I decided to revisit the library to find more information about Jikoya and its effects. The internet had provided some answers, but I needed a deeper understanding. I needed to know if others had experienced similar visions and what they had done about it.

The library was quiet, a stark contrast to the turmoil in my mind. I browsed through the shelves, picking up books on hallucinogens, brain chemistry, and dream interpretation. As I read, I found accounts of people experiencing vivid, life-like dreams after using similar substances. Some described feeling like seeing dream again using the drug.

One book caught my attention. It was an old, worn-out volume titled "Exploring the Subconscious: A Journey Through Dreams." The author, Dr. Ravindra Mehta, had dedicated his life to studying altered states of consciousness. I hoped his insights could shed some light on my experiences.

I spent hours engrossed in Dr. Mehta's book, absorbing his theories and findings. He believed that certain substances could unlock hidden parts of the brain, allowing individuals to access deeper layers of their subconscious. These experiences were not just random hallucinations but could reveal profound truths about one's inner self and even connect to other realms of existence.

Dr. Mehta's theories resonated with me. The visions I had seen while under the influence of Jikoya felt too real to be mere figments of my imagination. They seemed to hold a deeper significance, as if I had glimpsed into another world or dimension. I couldn't dismiss the possibility that my seizures and these visions were connected in some way.

I took notes as I read, jotting down anything that seemed relevant or insightful. Dr. Mehta wrote about the brain's ability to tap into alternate realities, suggesting that substances like Jikoya could act as a bridge between different planes of existence. It was a fascinating idea, one that made me question the nature of reality itself

## *Seeking Answers*

The library's quiet atmosphere allowed me to lose myself in the pages of the book. I read about ancient cultures that used similar substances in their rituals, believing they could communicate with their inner self. The parallels to my own experience were striking, and I felt a strange kinship with those who had walked this path before me.

As I delved deeper, I found accounts of people who had experienced living a previous dream after using substances like Jikoya. They described feeling a sense of unity with the universe, a connection to a higher consciousness that transcended their physical bodies.

I spent hours in the library, pouring over books and taking notes. The more I read, the more I felt like I was on the brink of a significant discovery. The connection between my seizures, the visions, and the substance Jikoya seemed undeniable, but I needed to understand how it all fit together.

As the afternoon turned into evening, I gathered my notes and the books I had borrowed, my mind buzzing with new information and theories. The journey to understand my experiences was just beginning, but I felt a sense of purpose and determination.

I returned home, my family already gathered for dinner. They asked about my day, and I told them I had been at the library, researching for a school project. It wasn't entirely a lie, but I knew they wouldn't understand the true nature of my quest.

After dinner, I retreated to my room, eager to continue my research. I spread out my notes and books on my desk, trying to piece together the puzzle. The more I read, the more I felt I was on the brink of a significant discovery. The connection between my seizures, the visions, and the substance Jikoya seemed undeniable, but I needed to understand how it all fit together.

## *Delving Deeper*

I spent the next few days immersed in my research. I read everything I could find on altered states of consciousness, dream interpretation, and hallucinogenic substances. The library became my second home, a sanctuary where I could explore the mysteries of my mind without interruption.

Dr. Mehta's book became my guide, his theories and insights providing a framework for understanding my experiences. He wrote about the brain's potential to access different dimensions of reality, suggesting that our perception of the world was just one layer of a much more complex and interconnected existence.

One passage in particular stood out to me: "The mind is a vast, unexplored frontier, capable of reaching beyond the confines of our physical reality. Through altered states of consciousness, we can glimpse the hidden truths that lie beneath the surface, connecting with realms and dimensions that defy our understanding."

These words resonated deeply with me. They echoed the sense of connection and belonging I had felt during my hallucinations, as if I were tapping into something far greater than myself. The idea that my seizures and the visions they brought were not just random events but part of a larger, interconnected reality was both exhilarating and daunting.

## *Confronting My Fears*

However, with each new discovery came a growing sense of fear and uncertainty. The more I learned, the more I realized how little I understood. The visions, the seizures, the connection to another world – it was all so far beyond my comprehension that I often felt overwhelmed and lost.

I knew I needed to confront my fears and uncertainties head-on. The experience with Jikoya had opened a door, and I couldn't ignore it any longer. I needed to understand what was happening to me and why.

One night, as I lay in bed, I stared at the ceiling, my mind racing with thoughts and questions. I couldn't sleep, my thoughts too loud and insistent. I kept replaying the events of the previous night in my mind, the vivid hallucinations and the overwhelming sensations.

The packet of Jikoya was still hidden in my drawer, a constant reminder of the path I had chosen. I knew that if I wanted to find answers, I would need to take the risk again. The substance had unlocked something within me, and I needed to explore it further.

## Chapter - 9
# Deeper Hallucinations

### *The School Routine*

Life seemed to fall back into its regular pattern, but beneath the surface, everything felt different. My school routine continued as usual, but it was as if I were living in two worlds at once. The mundane activities of everyday life felt surreal, almost detached from my consciousness. I attended classes, interacted with my friends, and participated in school activities, but there was an underlying current of something else, something that pulled at my attention constantly.

Every morning, I walked the familiar path to school, my footsteps echoing in the early light. The streets were the same, the faces were the same, but everything seemed to carry an otherworldly tint. It was as if the experiences with Jikoya had opened a door in my mind that could not be closed. The air felt charged with energy, and I was acutely aware of every sound and movement around me.

As I sat in my classes, my mind would drift. I found it hard to focus on the lessons being taught. My teachers' voices seemed distant, their words muffled by the persistent hum of my thoughts. I would look out the window, the green of the trees and the blue of the sky reminding me of Three Astral. It was as if the two worlds were superimposed on each other, and I was caught in the middle. The vibrant colors of Three Astral seemed to bleed into the dullness of my classroom, making it hard to distinguish where one world ended and the other began.

During recess, I would find myself gravitating towards the same old tree I always sat under. It had become my sanctuary, a place where I could escape the hustle and bustle of the playground and try to find some semblance of peace. But even there, I couldn't escape the feeling that I was being watched, that the tree itself was aware of my presence in a way that defied logic. The rustling of the leaves sounded like whispers, and the dappled sunlight created patterns on the ground that seemed to shift and move of their own accord.

One day, while sitting under the tree, I closed my eyes and tried to center myself. I focused on my breathing, attempting to ground myself in the present moment. But as I sat there, I began to feel a strange sensation, as if the tree's roots were extending towards me, seeking to connect with my own. The feeling was both comforting and unsettling, and I opened my eyes abruptly, breaking the spell.

### *Unsettling Hallucinations*

The hallucinations began to intrude more frequently. At first, they were subtle – a flicker of movement at the edge of my vision, a whispering sound that seemed to come from nowhere. But soon, they became more vivid and unsettling. I would see the vibrant colors of Three Astral overlaying the dullness of my school. The desks and chairs would morph into strange, living shapes, pulsating with energy. The walls seemed to breathe, expanding and contracting as if the entire building were alive.

One day, during a particularly monotonous math lesson, I glanced up from my notebook and saw the chalkboard come alive with swirling patterns and colors. The equations written in chalk transformed into intricate designs that seemed to pulse with life. I blinked, trying to clear my vision, but the patterns only grew more vivid, dancing before my eyes. The symbols seemed to speak to me in a language I couldn't understand, their meanings just out of reach.

In the hallways, the lockers would seem to shift and move, their metal surfaces reflecting strange, ethereal lights. I would hear faint whispers, as if the very walls were trying to communicate with me. It was both fascinating and terrifying, and I found it increasingly difficult to distinguish between reality and hallucination. The faces of my classmates appeared distorted, their features blending and shifting in a way that made it hard to recognize them.

During recess, I would sit under the shade of a tree, trying to ground myself in the present. But the tree would seem to come alive, its branches swaying and whispering to me in a language I couldn't understand. The grass beneath my feet felt like it was breathing, each blade pulsing with life. The world around me seemed to blur, the boundary between reality and hallucination becoming increasingly thin. I would reach out to touch the tree, feeling its bark warm and pulsating under my fingers, as if it had a heartbeat of its own.

The hallucinations were not confined to school. At home, they continued to plague me. The walls of my room seemed to close in on me, the posters and decorations morphing into strange, otherworldly scenes. My bed felt like it was floating, drifting through space and time. The sounds of the house – the creaking of the floorboards, the hum of the refrigerator – became amplified, transformed into a symphony of strange and unsettling noises.

## *A Strange New Sense*

It wasn't just the visual and auditory hallucinations that disturbed me. I began to feel an uncanny sense of connection to the plants and stones around me. It was as if I could sense their presence, their energy. The plants seemed to reach out to me, their leaves brushing against my skin with a sentience that was both comforting and terrifying. The stones under my feet felt alive, resonating with a deep, ancient power.

I would walk past the garden in the school courtyard and feel a pull, a magnetic attraction to the flowers and shrubs. Their colors were more vibrant, their scents more intoxicating. I felt as though I could communicate with them, understand their needs and desires. The stones along the pathway seemed to pulse with a steady, grounding energy, anchoring me to the earth.

One afternoon, I decided to test this newfound sense. I sat down by a cluster of flowers and closed my eyes, focusing on the sensation of their presence. As I breathed deeply, I could almost hear their voices, a soft, harmonious chorus that seemed to sing of growth and life. It was a beautiful and surreal experience, but it also left me feeling vulnerable and exposed.

This newfound sense was overwhelming. I didn't know how to process it, how to separate the hallucinations from reality. It was as if a part of Three Astral had followed me into my world, and I was powerless to stop it. The more I tried to ignore it, the stronger the sensations became.

## *Struggling with Reality*

The blurring of the lines between reality and hallucination began to take a toll on me. I found it harder and harder to concentrate on my schoolwork. My grades started to slip, and my teachers noticed my distracted state. They would call on me in class, but I would often be lost in my own world, unable to respond coherently.

My friends began to notice the change in me as well. They would ask if I was okay, if something was bothering me. I would brush off their concerns, not wanting to explain the strange and inexplicable experiences I was going through. How could I tell them that I was seeing and hearing things that weren't there, that I felt connected to the plants and stones in a way that defied all logic?

At home, I tried to maintain a sense of normalcy, but it was difficult. My parents were often busy with their own lives, and I didn't want to burden them with my troubles. My sister, who was usually my confidante, seemed distant, wrapped up in her own world. I felt isolated, trapped in a reality that I could no longer trust.

Every evening, I would retreat to my room, hoping to find some solace in the familiar surroundings. But even there, the hallucinations followed me. The posters on my walls seemed to come to life, the characters moving and speaking in ways they never had before. The ceiling would shift and change, transforming into a starry sky that reminded me of the vastness of Three Astral.

I tried to distract myself by reading or watching TV, but it was no use. The hallucinations were relentless, invading every aspect of my life. I couldn't escape them, couldn't find a moment of peace. It was as if my mind was a battlefield, and I was losing the fight to maintain my sanity.

## *A Desperate Decision*

One night, as I lay in bed, the weight of the hallucinations pressing down on me, I made a desperate decision. I couldn't continue living like this, caught between two worlds. The experiences with Jikoya had opened a door that I couldn't close, but I could choose not to walk through it again. I decided that I would never take Jikoya again.

The decision brought a sense of relief, but also a lingering fear. The substance had given me a glimpse into a world beyond my own, but it had also brought chaos and confusion into my life. I didn't know if I could handle the consequences of that choice, but I knew I had to try. I had to reclaim some semblance of normalcy, to find a way to ground myself in the reality I knew.

I spent the next few days trying to distance myself from the experiences that had consumed me. I focused on my schoolwork, forcing myself to pay attention in class and complete my assignments. It was a struggle, but I knew it was necessary. I had to prove to myself that I could still function, still live a normal life.

I avoided the places and things that triggered the hallucinations. I stopped sitting under the tree at recess, opting instead to stay in the bustling cafeteria where the noise and activity kept my mind occupied. I avoided the garden, the flowers and stones, anything that reminded me of the strange connection I felt.

But no matter how hard I tried, the hallucinations continued to haunt me. They were less frequent, but still present, lurking at the edges of my vision and consciousness. I began to fear that they would never go away, that I would always be trapped in this liminal space between reality and hallucination.

I began to meditate, hoping to calm my mind and find some inner peace. I would sit quietly in my room, focusing on my breath, letting go of the swirling thoughts and images. It wasn't easy, but slowly, I began to feel a sense of clarity. The hallucinations didn't disappear, but they became less overwhelming, less intrusive.

I also sought solace in nature, taking long walks in the park or along the river. The natural world had a calming effect on me, helping to ground me in the present moment. I would sit by the water, listening to the gentle lapping of the waves, and feel a sense of peace wash over me. The hallucinations seemed to fade into the background, allowing me to find some respite from the constant barrage of sensory overload.

Talking to my sister one evening, I opened up to her about the strange experiences I had been having. She listened patiently, her eyes filled with concern and understanding. She didn't judge me or dismiss my experiences, but offered her support and comfort. It was a relief to share my burden with someone, to know that I wasn't completely alone.

"Maybe you should talk to someone," she suggested gently. "A therapist or a counselor. They might be able to help you make sense of all this."

I nodded, considering her words. It was a daunting thought, opening up to a stranger about the bizarre and frightening experiences I was going through. But perhaps it was the next step in my journey towards understanding and healing.

As the days turned into weeks, I began to feel more grounded. The hallucinations still haunted me, but I was learning to navigate my way through them. I developed coping mechanisms, techniques to help me stay focused and present. I kept a journal, writing down my thoughts and experiences, trying to make sense of the chaos in my mind.

Through it all, I held on to the hope that I would find a way to reconcile the two worlds I was living in. The decision to never take Jikoya again was a pivotal moment in my journey.

## Chapter – 10
# Finally Taking the Drug Again to Understand the Connection

*Overwhelming Anxiety*

The days passed in a blur, each one more suffocating than the last. The hallucinations were relentless, invading my every waking moment. I couldn't escape them, couldn't find a shred of peace. My anxiety was through the roof, a constant hum in the back of my mind that I couldn't silence.

I felt like I was trapped in a nightmare, one that I couldn't wake up from. The vivid images of Three Astral were ever-present, overlaid on the mundane reality of my life. The plants and stones still whispered to me, their voices a constant reminder of the other world that seemed just out of reach. The once-familiar surroundings of my home and school now seemed alien and threatening, each shadow and corner hiding some new, terrifying vision.

Every morning, I would wake up with a sense of dread, knowing that the day ahead would be filled with hallucinations and anxiety. I would lie in bed, staring at the ceiling, trying to muster the energy to face the day. My body felt heavy, my mind foggy. The weight of the hallucinations was crushing, making it difficult to perform even the simplest tasks.

I would get dressed mechanically, my movements slow and deliberate. The clothes felt strange against my skin, as if they didn't belong to me. I would walk to the kitchen, the floorboards creaking under my feet, and try to eat breakfast. But food tasted like ash in my mouth, and the thought of swallowing made me nauseous. My appetite dwindled to almost nothing, and I began to lose weight. My family noticed the change, their concern growing with each passing day.

At school, things were no better. The classrooms that had once been a safe haven now felt like a prison. The teachers' voices seemed distant, their words distorted and unintelligible. I would sit at my desk, staring at the chalkboard, unable to focus on the lessons being taught. My classmates seemed to move in slow motion, their faces blurring and shifting in strange, unsettling ways.

During recess, I would isolate myself, seeking refuge under the shade of a tree. But even there, the hallucinations would follow me. The tree's branches would sway and whisper, their leaves rustling with secrets I couldn't understand. The grass beneath my feet felt alive, each blade pulsing with energy. The world around me seemed to blur, the boundary between reality and hallucination becoming increasingly thin.

My friends noticed the change in me, their concern evident in their eyes. They would ask if I was okay, if something was bothering me. But I couldn't bring myself to explain what was happening.

How could I tell them that I was seeing and hearing things that weren't there, that I felt connected to the plants and stones in a way that defied all logic?

Each day was a struggle to maintain some semblance of normalcy. I would try to engage in conversations, to participate in group activities, but my mind was always elsewhere. The images of Three Astral were ever-present, a constant reminder that I was living in two worlds at once. The plants and stones around me seemed to pulse with life, their energy mingling with my own. It was both exhilarating and terrifying, and I didn't know how to make sense of it all.

## *The Unbearable Curiosity*

Despite the fear and confusion, there was one emotion that overpowered all others: curiosity. I needed to know the truth. Were the visions and hallucinations a product of the Jikoya drug, or was there something more to them? Was Three Astral real, or was it all just a figment of my imagination?

The questions gnawed at me, day and night. I couldn't focus on anything else. The need for answers consumed me, driving me to the brink of desperation. I would lie awake at night, my mind racing with thoughts and theories. I replayed the events of my hallucinations over and over, searching for clues that might reveal the truth.

I tried to distract myself with schoolwork and hobbies, but nothing could hold my attention for long. The vivid images of Three Astral haunted me, pulling me back into that otherworldly realm. I would find myself daydreaming, lost in the vibrant landscapes and strange creatures of my visions. The line between reality and hallucination continued to blur, leaving me in a state of perpetual confusion.

One evening, as I sat in my room, I decided to write down everything I remembered about my experiences with Jikoya. I hoped that putting my thoughts on paper might help me make sense of them. I wrote for hours, filling pages with detailed descriptions of the hallucinations, the sensations, and the emotions I had felt. But the more I wrote, the more questions I had. The need for answers grew stronger, and I knew that there was only one way to get them.

I began to research everything I could find about hallucinogenic substances and their effects. I read books, scoured online forums, and watched videos of people sharing their experiences. But none of it seemed to match what I was going through. The accounts I found were full of strange and vivid hallucinations, but none of them described the sense of connection and belonging that I felt with Three Astral.

The more I read, the more I became convinced that my experiences were unique. It wasn't just the drug; there was something else at play. The visions felt too real, too consistent to be mere hallucinations. I began to wonder if I had stumbled upon something extraordinary, a gateway to another world.

But the thought of taking the drug again filled me with dread. The last experience had been overwhelming, nearly breaking me. I didn't know if I could handle it a second time. But the need for answers was stronger than my fear. I had to know.

## *The Perfect Opportunity*

As if the universe sensed my desperation, an opportunity presented itself. My family announced that they would be going to the village for a few days to sort out some property ownership legalities. I was to stay behind and take care of the house. It was the perfect chance. I would be alone, with no one to disturb me. No one to notice if something went wrong.

The night before they left, I could hardly sleep. My mind was racing, a mix of anticipation and fear. I kept thinking about the packet of Jikoya hidden in my drawer, the substance that held the key to my questions. I tried to calm myself, reminding myself that I had to be careful, that I couldn't let my anxiety get the better of me.

The next morning, I saw my family off, waving as they drove away. As soon as they were out of sight, I felt a strange mix of freedom and trepidation. The house was eerily quiet, the silence amplifying my thoughts. I went to my room, sat on my bed, and stared at the drawer where the Jikoya was hidden.

For hours, I sat there, unable to move. My mind was a whirlwind of conflicting emotions. I wanted to take the drug, to see the visions again, but I was terrified of what might happen. What if it was too much for me to handle? What if I lost myself in the hallucinations and couldn't come back?

But the need for answers was too strong. I had to know if Three Astral was real, if there was some deeper meaning to the hallucinations. I took a deep breath, trying to steady my trembling hands, and reached for the drawer.

I spent the next few hours preparing myself mentally. I took deep breaths, trying to calm my racing heart. I reminded myself of the reasons I was doing this, the need to understand the connection between my seizures and the otherworldly realm. I couldn't let fear hold me back.

### *The Moment of Decision*

For what felt like an eternity, I sat on the edge of my bed, staring at the packet of Jikoya. My mind was a whirlwind of conflicting emotions. I wanted to take the drug, to see the visions again, but I was terrified of what might happen. What if it was too much for me to handle? What if I lost myself in the hallucinations and couldn't come back?

But the need for answers was too strong. I had to know if Three Astral was real, if there was some deeper meaning to the hallucinations. I took a deep breath, trying to steady my trembling hands, and reached for the drawer.

I opened it slowly, my heart pounding in my chest. The packet of Jikoya seemed to glow in the dim light of my room, its presence both comforting and menacing. I took it out, my hands shaking, and placed it on the bed beside me. The small packet held so much power, the potential to unlock the secrets that had been tormenting me.

I knew the procedure. Crush the substance into a fine powder, place it on a spoon, and heat it until it turned into smoke. Then inhale the smoke and wait for the effects to take hold. I had done it before, and I could do it again. But this time, the stakes felt higher. I needed to be sure, to find the answers I was searching for.

I went through the motions mechanically, trying to keep my mind focused. Crush the powder. Place it on the spoon. Heat it with a lighter. The smoke rose, thin and wispy, filling the air with a pungent scent. I hesitated for a moment, my fear threatening to overtake me. But I pushed it aside, reminding myself why I was doing this. I needed answers.

Taking a deep breath, I brought the spoon to my lips and inhaled the smoke. It burned my throat and lungs, but I forced myself to take it all in. Almost immediately, I felt the familiar heaviness settle over me, my limbs growing numb. I lay back on the bed, staring at the ceiling as the effects of the Jikoya took hold.

The room around me began to fade, replaced by the vivid, surreal world of Three Astral. The colors were brighter, the sounds sharper, and the sensations more intense. It was as if I were stepping into another dimension, a place where the boundaries of reality no longer applied.

The transition was smoother this time, less jarring. I felt my consciousness expand, merging with the vibrant energies of Three Astral. The landscapes unfolded before me, a kaleidoscope of colors and shapes that defied description.

I could feel the life force of the plants and stones, their energy resonating with my own.

## *Turn To Chapter 7: Right Hand Side (Page no. 196)*

## Chapter – 11
# Hospitalization and Realizations

### *Waking Up in the Hospital*

I woke up to the sterile smell of antiseptics and the rhythmic beeping of machines. My head felt heavy, and my vision was blurry as I slowly opened my eyes. The white ceiling above me was unfamiliar, and it took me a few moments to realize I was in a hospital bed. My initial thought was that I had experienced another seizure, but as my senses sharpened, I heard voices nearby, and the reality of my situation began to sink in.

My parent's voices drifted through the curtain that separated my bed from the rest of the room. They were speaking in hushed tones, but their words were filled with stress and blame.

"It's because you didn't take proper care of him," my father accused, his voice low but angry.

"Don't you dare put this on me," my mother retorted, her voice shaking with frustration. "You know how difficult things have been."

Their argument faded into the background as I tried to piece together what had happened. The last thing I remembered was being in my room, overwhelmed by the hallucinations and the urge to take the Jikoya drug again.

My thoughts were interrupted by the sight of my sister approaching my bed.

"Tathastu," she said softly, her eyes filled with concern. "How are you feeling now?"

I tried to sit up, but my body felt weak. "I'm... I'm okay, I guess. I don't know when these seizures will stop."

She shook her head gently. "You weren't admitted because of a seizure this time. It's because of a high dose of drugs. We found you at home, almost lifeless. The doctors said it was a near-lethal dose. You've been unconscious for two days."

Her words hit me like a punch to the gut. I had been so consumed by my desperation to reconnect with the visions of Three Astral that I hadn't considered the physical toll it was taking on my body. I watched as my sister walked away, leaving me alone with my thoughts.

Lying in that hospital bed, my mind was a whirlwind of conflicting thoughts and emotions. My parent's argument continued to echo in my head, their words a constant reminder of the tightness and blame that surrounded my condition. How could I explain to them what I was experiencing? How could I make them understand the connection I felt to another world, another reality?

As I stared at the ceiling, questions began to flood my mind. Why did my parents seem to care so much now, when they had been so distant before? Would they ever forgive me if they knew the truth about the drugs? And then there was Lika, the enigmatic figure from my visions.

Should I help her, and if so, how could I do that from here?

The more I thought about Lika and the plight of Three Astral, the more restless I became. The visions had felt so real, so urgent. But now, lying in this hospital bed, everything seemed distant and hazy. I needed clarity, and I was desperate to understand what was happening to me.

My mind was racing, unable to find peace. The craving for the drug, for the connection to the visions, was almost unbearable. I needed to know what had happened on Three Astral, to understand my role in that world and how it intersected with my reality on Earth. The doctors had taken the Jikoya drug away, and I knew that even if I found a way to get it again, it would only lead to more trouble.

I closed my eyes, trying to focus on the memories of my time in Three Astral. The images of Lika, the green core, and the struggle against dark matter flooded my mind. I remembered the sense of purpose I felt there, the belief that I could make a difference. But here, in the hospital, that sense of purpose seemed out of reach.

As I lay there, I realized that I couldn't keep this secret any longer. The weight of it was too much to bear alone. But how could I explain something so unbelievable to my family? How could I make them understand that my seizures were more than just medical episodes, that they were a bridge to another world?

The thought of their reactions terrified me. Would they think I was crazy? Would they blame themselves even more for my condition? The fear of their judgment kept me silent, but the need to share my experiences was growing stronger.

I thought about my sister's words, about how they had found me nearly dead from the overdose. The guilt of putting my family through that was overwhelming. I needed to find a way to make them understand, to help them see the bigger picture. But first, I needed to come to terms with it myself.

Days passed, and my physical strength slowly returned. My parents visited frequently, their faces lined with worry and fatigue. Each visit was filled with questions I couldn't answer, and the weight of my secret grew heavier with each passing day.

One afternoon, as my father sat beside my bed, I decided it was time to confront my fear. "Dad," I began, my voice trembling. "There's something I need to tell you."

He looked at me, his eyes filled with concern. "What is it, Tathastu?"

I took a deep breath, trying to steady my nerves. "The seizures... they're not just medical episodes. There's more to it. When I have a seizure, I see things. I see another world, another life. And it's so real, Dad. I can't explain it, but I feel like I'm meant to be there."

My father's expression shifted from concern to confusion. "What are you talking about?"

I hesitated, unsure of how to explain. "There's a place called Three Astral. It's a world with core elements and beings that I've never seen before. And there's a girl named Lika. She needs my help."

He stared at me, his brow furrowing. "Tathastu, are you saying this is all real?"

"I don't know, Dad," I admitted, my voice breaking. "But it feels real. And I can't shake the feeling that I'm supposed to do something important there."

My father's eyes softened as he reached out to take my hand. "Son, I don't fully understand what you're going through. But I believe you. And we'll find a way to help you, whatever it takes."

Tears welled up in my eyes as I squeezed his hand. "Thank you, Dad. I just need you to believe in me."

He nodded, his grip firm and reassuring. "We'll get through this together, Tathastu. You're not alone."

For the first time in what felt like forever, I felt a glimmer of hope. The road ahead was uncertain, but with my family's support, I knew I could face whatever challenges lay ahead.

### *The Weight of Realizations*

The more I thought about Lika and the plight of Three Astral, the more restless I became. The visions had felt so real, so urgent. But now, lying in this hospital bed, everything seemed distant and hazy. I needed clarity, and I was desperate to understand what was happening to me.

The constant beeping of the machines around me served as a harsh reminder of my physical state. My body felt weak and frail, a stark contrast to the vibrant and powerful being I had felt like in my visions. I wondered if I would ever feel that sense of purpose again, or if I was doomed to be trapped in this cycle of confusion and despair.

The doctors and nurses came and went, their faces a blur of concern and professionalism. They asked me questions about my physical state, about my drug use, about the events leading up to my hospitalization. But I couldn't bring myself to tell them the full truth. How could I explain something so unbelievable, so surreal?

The weight of my secret was crushing. I felt isolated, even as my family tried to support me. I could see the worry in their eyes, the fear that they might lose me. And I couldn't blame them. I had put them through so much already. The guilt was overwhelming, and I didn't know how much longer I could keep it all inside.

One evening, as the sun set outside the hospital window, casting long shadows across the room, my sister came to visit. She sat beside my bed, her expression soft and understanding. "Tathastu," she began, her voice gentle. "I know things have been really hard for you. And I want you to know that we're all here for you, no matter what."

I nodded, unable to find the words to respond. She reached out and took my hand, her touch warm and reassuring. "Whatever you're going through, you don't have to go through it alone. We're your family, and we'll do whatever it takes to help you get through this."

Tears welled up in my eyes, and I squeezed her hand tightly. "Thank you," I whispered, my voice breaking. "I just... I don't know how to explain what's happening to me."

She smiled softly, her eyes filled with empathy. "You don't have to explain it all right now. Just take it one step at a time. We'll figure it out together."

For the first time in what felt like forever, I felt a glimmer of hope. The road ahead was uncertain, but with my family's support, I knew I could face whatever challenges lay ahead. I wasn't alone, and that made all the difference.

## *The Craving for Answers*

As the days turned into weeks, my physical strength slowly began to return. But with each passing day, the craving for answers grew stronger. The visions of Three Astral, the memories of Lika and the green core, were always at the forefront of my mind. I needed to understand what was happening to me, to find some sense of clarity in the midst of the chaos.

One afternoon, as my mother sat beside my bed, I decided it was time to confront my fear. My heart raced as I gathered the courage to speak. "Mom," I began, my voice trembling and eyes cast downward, "there's something I need to tell you."

She looked at me with a mixture of concern and love, her eyes searching mine for answers. "What is it, Tathastu?" she asked softly, her voice soothing yet filled with worry.

I took a deep breath, trying to steady my nerves, feeling the weight of my secret pressing down on me. "The seizures... they're not just medical episodes. There's more to it. When I have a seizure, I see things. I see another world, another life. And it's so real, Mom. I can't explain it, but I feel like I'm meant to be there."

Her expression shifted to one of confusion and disbelief. "What do you mean, another world?" she asked, her brow furrowing as she tried to grasp the meaning of my words.

I hesitated, struggling to find the right words. "There's a place called Three Astral. It's unlike anything we've ever seen here. It's a world filled with core elements and beings that defy explanation. And there's a girl named Lika. She needs my help."

My mother stared at me, her face a mix of concern and bewilderment. "Tathastu, are you saying this is all real?" she asked, her voice tinged with skepticism.

"I don't know, Mom," I admitted, my voice breaking as tears welled up in my eyes. "But it feels real. Every time I have a seizure, I'm transported to this place. It's so vivid, so tangible. And I can't shake the feeling that I'm supposed to do something important there."

She reached out and took my hand in hers, her touch warm and reassuring. "Son, I don't fully understand what you're going through. But I believe you," she said, her eyes brimming with empathy and determination. "We'll find a way to help you, whatever it takes."

Her words brought a flood of emotions, and I squeezed her hand tightly, feeling a surge of gratitude and relief. "Thank you, Mom. I just need you to believe in me," I whispered, my voice choked with emotion.

She nodded, her grip firm and unwavering. "We'll get through this together, Tathastu. You're not alone," she promised, her voice strong and filled with conviction.

In that moment, I felt a glimmer of hope for the first time in what seemed like forever. The road ahead was uncertain, fraught with challenges and unknowns, but with my family's support, I knew I could face whatever lay ahead.

As we sat there, my mother began to share stories from her own life, moments when she had felt lost or scared, and how she had overcome those challenges. Her words were a balm to my soul, a reminder that I was not alone in my struggles. She spoke of times when our family had faced adversity, and how we had always found a way through, together.

"Do you remember when your father lost his job?" she asked, her voice soft but steady. "We were so scared, wondering how we would make ends meet. But we stuck together, and we made it through. This is no different, Tathastu. We will find a way."

Her stories filled me with a sense of resilience, a belief that I could overcome the obstacles before me. She held my hand throughout, her presence a constant source of strength.

As the afternoon turned into evening, my mother and I continued to talk, our bond growing stronger with each shared word. She helped me see that my visions of Three Astral, whether real or imagined, were a part of my journey, a part of who I was becoming.

By the time the sun dipped below the horizon, casting a warm glow through my bedroom window, I felt a newfound determination. My mother's unwavering support had ignited a spark within me, a belief that I could face the unknown and find my place in the world, whether it was here or in Three Astral.

"Thank you, Mom," I said again, my voice steady now, filled with gratitude and hope. "I don't know what the future holds, but with you by my side, I know I can face it."

She smiled, her eyes shining with love and pride. "We'll face it together, Tathastu. Whatever comes, we'll face it together."

However, deep down, I knew she wasn't entirely convinced. She was agreeing with me because I wasn't well, because she couldn't bear to see me suffer alone. There was a flicker of doubt in her eyes, a hesitation that she tried to mask with her reassuring words. I could feel her fear, her uncertainty. But in that moment, her love for me overshadowed everything else. She was willing to put aside her doubts to support me, to be there for me. And that meant more to me than anything.

## Chapter - 12
# Sister Helps Me Get That Drug

### *The Burden of Thoughts*

The days after my last hospital visit were a blur. My mind was a chaotic swirl of thoughts and emotions. The vivid hallucinations and the ever-present voices of the plants around me had become overwhelming. I felt like I was losing my grip on reality, and the weight of it all was suffocating. I was consumed by the need to understand what was happening to me, and the memories of Three Astral haunted my every waking moment.

I found myself acting out of character, my behavior becoming more erratic and unpredictable. My family noticed the changes, but they didn't understand the root of my distress. I felt isolated, trapped in my own mind, unable to share the full extent of my experiences with anyone. The burden of my secret was becoming too much to bear.

One afternoon, as I sat in my room staring blankly at the ceiling, my sister walked in. She had always been perceptive, and she could see that something was deeply troubling me. Her concern was palpable, and I knew I couldn't keep this from her any longer.

"Tathastu," she said gently, sitting down beside me. "What's going on? You've been acting so strange lately. I'm worried about you."

I looked at her, my eyes filling with tears. "I don't even know where to start," I said, my voice trembling. "It's all so confusing, and I feel like I'm losing my mind."

"Just tell me, "She urged. "Whatever it is, you can tell me. I'm here for you."

### *Confession and Tears*

Taking a deep breath, I began to explain everything to her. I told her about the strange visions, the feeling that everything around me was alive and speaking to me. I described the dreams in which I saw myself on a different planet, becoming another being during my seizure attacks. I recounted how the inhabitants of Three Astral had told me that I became alive on their planet whenever I suffered a seizure on Earth.

As I spoke, the tears flowed freely. I was crying not just because of the fear and confusion, but also because of the immense relief of finally sharing my secret with someone. My sister listened intently, her expression a mixture of concern and disbelief.

"I don't know what to do," I said, my voice breaking. "I feel like I'm going crazy. I need to understand these dreams, to know if they're real or just my mind playing tricks on me. I need Jikoya to make sense of it all."

She reached out and took my hand, her grip firm and reassuring. "Tathastu, I need you to promise me that everything you're telling me is true. I need to know that you're not making this up."

"I promise," I said, my voice filled with desperation. "I swear it's all true. I wouldn't lie about something like this."

She looked deep into my eyes, searching for any sign of deception. Finally, she nodded. "Alright, I believe you. And I want to help you. But you have to promise me that you'll be careful, that you won't let this consume you."

"I promise," I said, my heart pounding with a mixture of hope and fear. "I just need to understand what's happening to me."

### *The Plan*

My sister took a deep breath, her mind already working on a plan. "Okay, give me some time. I'll get the Jikoya from your room. But you have to promise me that you'll only use it to find answers, not to escape from reality."

"I promise," I said, feeling a surge of gratitude and relief. "Thank you. I don't know what I'd do without you."

She nodded, giving me a reassuring smile. "We're in this together, Tathastu. We'll figure it out."

She left the room, and I sat there, my heart racing with anticipation. The thought of taking Jikoya again filled me with a mixture of fear and excitement. I knew the risks, but I was desperate for answers. The memories of Three Astral and the mystery of Lika's plea for help consumed my thoughts.

As I waited for my sister to return, I tried to calm my racing mind. I knew that taking Jikoya again was dangerous, but I felt like I had no other choice. I needed to know what was real and what wasn't. I needed to understand my connection to Three Astral and my role in its fate.

### *The Moment of Truth*

It felt like an eternity before my sister returned, holding a small, familiar vial in her hand. She handed it to me, her eyes filled with a mix of fear and determination. "Here it is," she said softly. "Please be careful."

I took the vial from her, my hands trembling. "Thank you," I whispered. "I will."

She watched as I prepared the Jikoya, crushing it into a fine powder and placing it on a spoon. The ritual felt both familiar and terrifying. As I heated the spoon and the smoke began to rise, I felt a wave of fear wash over me. But I pushed it aside, knowing that I needed to do this.

With my sister by my side, I inhaled the smoke, feeling the drug take effect almost immediately. The world around me began to blur, and I felt a familiar sensation of detachment from my body. I lay back on my bed, my eyes fixed on the ceiling as the room around me faded away.

### *The Transition*

As the effects of the drug deepened, I felt myself being pulled into a different reality. The room around me dissolved, replaced by a swirling vortex of colors and shapes. I closed my eyes, surrendering to the sensation as I felt myself being transported to another place.

When I opened my eyes again, I found myself standing in the midst of a lush, vibrant landscape. The air was filled with the scent of blooming flowers, and the sky above was a brilliant shade of green... It was Three Astral, the world I had seen in my visions.

I looked down at my hands, expecting to see my own familiar form. But instead, I saw the hands of another being, just as I had seen in my dreams. The realization hit me with a jolt—I was Kenyzee once again.

As I took in my surroundings, a sense of clarity washed over me. The memories of my previous experiences in Three Astral flooded back, and I knew that this was no mere dream. This was real, and I had a purpose here.

I turned to see Lika approaching, her face filled with relief and joy. "Kenyzee," she said softly, her voice filled with emotion.

## *Turn To Chapter 11: Right Hand Side (Page no. 230)*

## Chapter – 13
# Dream End, Tried Jikoya but Can't See Anything

### *Waking Up in Desperation*

I woke up with a start, my heart pounding and my mind in a whirlwind. "Lika!" I screamed, sitting up abruptly. As my eyes adjusted to the dim light, I realized I was back in my room on Earth. The familiar surroundings felt alien after the vivid experiences on Three Astral. I could still feel the lingering effects of the Jikoya drug, but the dream had ended abruptly, leaving me in a state of desperate confusion.

The walls of my room seemed to close in on me as I struggled to make sense of what had happened. The posters of my favorite bands, the cluttered desk with unfinished homework, and the pile of clothes on the chair felt like relics from another life. I had been so immersed in the world of Three Astral that returning to my earthly reality felt jarring and disorienting.

I glanced around, trying to ground myself, but my mind kept drifting back to the final moments of my dream. I could still hear Lika's voice, see the chaotic energy swirling around us, and feel the weight of my failure to stabilize the core elements. The desperation to know what had happened consumed me.

The remnants of the Jikoya drug lay on the bedside table, a stark reminder of the lengths I had gone to connect with that other world. My hands trembled as I reached for it, my mind racing with questions. Did I manage to save Lika? Was the planet stabilizing? Or had my efforts been in vain?

With trembling hands, I started preparing the Jikoya drug once more. The process felt mechanical, my movements driven by sheer desperation. I crushed the remnants of the drug into a fine powder, placed it on a spoon, and held it over a candle flame until it began to smoke. I inhaled deeply, hoping to reconnect with the memories and the world of Three Astral.

The familiar sensation washed over me, and for a moment, I felt a flicker of hope. But once again, I saw only my memories up to the point where I screamed Lika's name. Beyond that, there was nothing but a frustrating blank. The sense of loss and confusion was overwhelming. It was as if the connection had been severed, leaving me stranded between two worlds.

### *Desperate for Answers*

The room around me felt suffocating as I sat there, alone with my thoughts. The familiar sights of my earthly belongings did little to comfort me. Anxiety clawed at my insides, and I felt an overwhelming urge to understand why my memories were cut off at that crucial moment.

I tried to calm my racing mind and think logically. I remembered that my seizures had a direct correlation with my experiences on Three Astral. The seizures lasted for about 166 seconds, and from my calculations, one second on Earth equaled a full day on Three Astral. I started counting the days from my memories and realized that the last moment I recalled on Three Astral was exactly at the 166-day mark.

This realization hit me hard. It meant that Kenyzee could no longer act or do anything because my frequency wasn't aligned with his. To reawaken Kenyzee, I needed to trigger another seizure. The urgency to reconnect with Three Astral and find out what had happened to Lika gnawed at me relentlessly.

Desperation drove me to turn to the internet. I spent hours searching for ways to trigger a seizure safely. The options were limited and risky, but my desperation overrode my caution. I found a few methods that seemed plausible, including sleep deprivation and intense strobe lights.

The room was filled with the dim glow of my computer screen as I scoured forums and medical websites. Each method I found seemed more dangerous than the last, but I was willing to try anything. I needed to know what had happened on Three Astral. The thought of Lika and the people depending on me drove me to push past my fears.

### *Searching for a Solution*

Determined to reestablish the connection, I turned to the internet. I spent hours searching for ways to trigger a seizure safely. The options were limited and risky, but my desperation overrode my caution. I found a few methods that seemed plausible, including sleep deprivation and intense strobe lights.

I decided to try the sleep deprivation method first. I stayed awake for over 48 hours, pushing my body to the brink of exhaustion. The hallucinations from the lack of sleep only added to my anxiety. I felt my body weakening, but there was no sign of an impending seizure.

Next, I tried using intense strobe lights. I set up the lights in my room, hoping the flickering patterns would trigger a seizure. I stared into the lights, my eyes straining against the harsh, repetitive flashes. Minutes felt like hours as I waited, but nothing happened.

Frustration and despair began to set in. I needed to trigger a seizure, but my body seemed uncooperative. I turned to other methods mentioned in the forums, including hyperventilation and inducing stress. I tried everything, pushing my body to its limits. The fear of failing Lika and the people of Three Astral drove me to continue despite the risks.

After several more failed attempts, I decided to combine all the methods. I stayed awake for another 24 hours, then used the strobe lights while hyperventilating. My body felt like it was on the edge of collapse. The world around me started to blur, and I felt a familiar sensation creeping in. Finally, my body gave in.

### *Triggering a Seizure*

Frustration and despair began to set in. I needed to trigger a seizure, but my body seemed uncooperative. I turned to other methods mentioned in the forums, including hyperventilation and inducing stress. I tried everything, pushing my body to its limits. The fear of failing Lika and the people of Three Astral drove me to continue despite the risks.

After several more failed attempts, I decided to combine all the methods. I stayed awake for another 24 hours, then used the strobe lights while hyperventilating. My body felt like it was on the edge of collapse. The world around me started to blur, and I felt a familiar sensation creeping in. Finally, my body gave in.

I woke up in a hospital bed, the beeping of monitors surrounding me. I felt a mixture of relief and confusion. My body ached, and my head throbbed. I saw my dad sitting beside me, his face etched with worry. "You had another seizure," he said, his voice a mix of concern and confusion. "We found you unconscious in your room."

Despite the pain and the fatigue, a wave of happiness washed over me. The seizure meant I had reconnected with Three Astral. I couldn't help but smile, but my reaction drew concerned looks from the hospital staff and my dad. They didn't understand the significance of what had happened.

As I lay there, my mind raced with anticipation. I needed to know what had happened on Three Astral. Did my efforts make a difference? Was Lika safe? These questions fueled my determination to continue, no matter the risks. I knew that my journey was far from over, and the fate of Two Astral still hung in the balance.

However, a nagging thought lingered at the back of my mind. Had I been able to stabilize the core elements and save Lika, or had my actions fallen short? The uncertainty gnawed at me, and I knew that I would have to find out, even if it meant putting myself at risk again. The answers were out there, waiting for me in the realm of Three Astral.

## Chapter - 14
# Back to Home

### *Returning Home*

I came back home from the hospital, my mind still buzzing with the fragmented memories of Three Astral and the desperation to know what had happened to Lika and the planet. The antiseptic smell of the hospital clung to me, a stark contrast to the familiar scents of home. As I stepped into the house, the usual comfort of being back felt overshadowed by the weight of unanswered questions.

The house was quiet, with my parents preoccupied in their own worlds and my sister engrossed in her studies. I made my way to my room, the place that had once been my sanctuary now felt like a prison. I needed to reconnect with Three Astral, to see if my efforts had made any difference. But as I searched my room, I realized that I had used the last dose of Jikoya. The sense of urgency and desperation grew stronger with each passing moment.

I sat on my bed, my mind racing. The need to understand what had happened to Lika and the stability of Three Astral was overwhelming. The memory of her tearful goodbye haunted me, and I knew I couldn't rest until I had answers. The thought of returning to the dark web filled me with a mixture of dread and determination. It was a risky endeavor, but I had no other choice. The pull to understand was too strong to ignore.

I logged onto my computer, my fingers trembling as I navigated to the dark web once more. The screen's glow cast eerie shadows in my room, adding to the stress. I remembered the peril of my previous encounter and resolved to be more cautious this time. I needed to ensure the transaction went smoothly without attracting unwanted attention.

### *Venturing into the Dark Web*

Navigating the dark web felt like stepping into a shadowy underworld. The anonymity and secrecy of the platform made it both dangerous and alluring. I scrolled through the various listings, searching for a vendor who could provide me with Jikoya. My previous encounter had been harrowing, and I was determined to be more cautious this time.

The hours seemed to stretch endlessly as I sifted through numerous vendors. Each profile was scrutinized, every review read meticulously. Trust was a scarce commodity in this clandestine marketplace. Finally, I found a vendor who promised a discreet delivery. The vendor's profile had positive reviews, and the transactions appeared to be legitimate. I messaged the vendor, carefully negotiating the terms of the deal. This time, the vendor offered to deliver the package to a nearby post office, which seemed safer than meeting in person.

The days leading up to the delivery were filled with anxiety. I couldn't shake the fear that the package would be intercepted or that something would go wrong. Each night, I lay awake, my mind racing with thoughts of what I might find when I reconnected with Three Astral. The anticipation was almost unbearable. I double-checked the delivery instructions, making sure everything was in order. My heart pounded each time I received a notification, fearing it might be related to the package.

## *The Package Arrives*

Finally, the day arrived. I received a notification that the package had been delivered to the post office. My heart pounded as I made my way there, the fear of being discovered gnawing at me. The post office was bustling with activity, and I tried to blend in, hoping not to draw any attention.

I approached the counter, my hands trembling as I handed over my ID. The clerk barely glanced at it before retrieving the package. Relief washed over me as I took the package and hurried out of the building, my heart still racing. The entire process had gone smoothly, but the real challenge was yet to come.

Back home, I waited until everyone was asleep. The quiet of the house amplified the pounding of my heart as I carefully opened the package. Inside was the familiar vial of Jikoya. I took a deep breath, steeling myself for what was to come. I knew the risks, but my desperation to reconnect with Three Astral overrode any fear.

The weight of the package felt heavier than it should, as if it contained not just the drug but the answers to all my questions. I hid it carefully, waiting for the right moment to use it. The anxiety and anticipation built up, making every passing hour feel like an eternity. The night finally fell, and I could hear the soft snores of my family, signaling it was time.

### *Preparing the Jikoya*

I went up to the terrace, the cool night air providing a stark contrast to the tightness boiling inside me. The stars above seemed indifferent to my plight, twinkling serenely as I prepared the Jikoya. I crushed the remnants of the drug into a fine powder, placed it on a spoon, and held it over a candle flame until it began to smoke.

The familiar ritual felt both comforting and terrifying. I inhaled deeply, hoping to reconnect with the memories and the world of Three Astral. The smoke filled my lungs, and I closed my eyes, willing myself to see beyond the blank void that had plagued my previous attempts.

The initial rush was familiar, a mix of euphoria and anticipation. My senses heightened, and I felt a slight disconnect from the physical world. I braced myself for the journey ahead, hoping it would bring the clarity I so desperately sought. I focused on the last memory, the scream for Lika, and waited for the visions to unfold.

### *The Pain of Separation*

For a moment, there was nothing but darkness. Then, slowly, images began to form. I saw Lika, her eyes filled with tears. She was saying goodbye, her voice choked with emotion. "Goodbye, Kenyzee," she whispered. The sight of her tear-streaked face tore at my heart. I couldn't hold back the tears that streamed down my own face. The connection was fleeting, but the impact was profound.

The images faded, and I was left staring at the night sky, my heart heavy with grief and confusion. The drug had given me a glimpse, but it was not enough. I needed to know more. The sight of Lika's tears haunted me, and I couldn't shake the feeling that I had failed her.

I sat on the terrace, the cool breeze doing little to soothe the turmoil inside me. The world around me felt distant and unreal. My thoughts were consumed by the brief vision of Lika and the unanswered questions that gnawed at my soul.

Why had she said goodbye? What had happened after our last encounter? The uncertainty was unbearable. I knew I had to find a way to reconnect with Three Astral, to understand the events that had transpired. But the path forward was unclear, and the risks were immense.

As I sat there, the weight of my responsibility pressed down on me. The lives of everyone on Three Astral depended on my actions, and I couldn't afford to fail. The journey ahead was fraught with danger, but I was determined to see it through.

The night wore on, and I remained on the terrace, lost in thought. The enormity of the task before me was daunting, but I couldn't give up. The fate of an entire world hung in the balance, and I was their only hope.

As the first light of dawn began to creep over the horizon, I made a silent vow. I would find a way to reconnect with Three Astral, to understand what had happened and to save Lika and her world. No matter the cost, I would not rest until I had answers.

I wondered whether I had been able to stabilize the core elements and save Lika or not. The suspense of not knowing gnawed at my soul, leaving me in a state of perpetual anxiety and determination. The connection between my life on Earth and the fate of Three Astral was now inextricably linked, and I had no choice but to pursue the truth, no matter where it led me.

## Chapter - 15
# Final Move

### *The Decision*

The weight of uncertainty and desperation pressed heavily on me. The fragmentary glimpses of Three Astral, the fleeting image of Lika, and the gnawing questions left me with no other choice. I needed answers, and I was willing to take the ultimate risk to get them. I stared at the remaining Jikoya, knowing what I had to do.

I gathered all the remaining Jikoya, feeling the gravity of my decision. My hands trembled as I prepared the drug one last time. I crushed the entire contents into a fine powder, aware that consuming it all at once was incredibly dangerous. But the thought of leaving things unresolved was unbearable. I took a deep breath, steeling myself for what was to come.

### *Consuming the Jikoya*

I inhaled deeply, consuming all the Jikoya at once. The potent mixture burned through my lungs, and I felt an immediate, overwhelming sensation. My body began to tingle, then slowly become numb. The room around me started to blur and fade, the edges of my vision darkening as the drug took full effect.

The numbness spread rapidly, and I felt myself slipping away from the physical world. My heart pounded erratically, and my breathing became shallow. Despite the fear and pain, a strange sense of calm washed over me. This was it—the final move. I was all in.

### *Transitioning*

The world around me dissolved into darkness, a void of silence and stillness. For a moment, I felt nothing but an eerie calm, as if I were floating in an abyss. Then, slowly, light began to seep into the darkness, and I felt a familiar tug, pulling me toward a different reality.

Images started to form, hazy at first, then sharpening into focus. I could see the vibrant colors of Three Astral, the swirling energies of the core elements, and the breathtaking landscapes. I felt the ground solidify beneath my feet, the air filling my lungs with a sense of familiarity.

### *Arrival on Three Astral*

As the last remnants of the darkness faded away, I found myself standing on Three Astral. The vibrant, surreal landscape stretched out before me, and I could feel the energies of the core elements pulsating around me. The sensation was overwhelming, but it was also comforting. I was back.

---

## *Turn To Chapter 15: Right Hand Side (Page no. 268)*

---

## Chapter - 16
# Real Truth

### *The Revelation*

The sterile white walls of the hospital room felt suffocating as I lay there, staring blankly at the ceiling. The beeping of the monitors was the only sound, a rhythmic reminder of my current state. My family was gathered around me, their faces etched with worry and confusion. I knew it was time to share the truth, no matter how unbelievable it sounded.

"Mom, Dad, there's something I need to tell you," I began, my voice shaky but resolute. My parents exchanged worried glances, and my sister stepped closer, holding my hand.

"What is it, Tathastu?" my mother asked, her voice tinged with concern.

Taking a deep breath, I launched into the story of my experiences on Three Astral. I told them about Lika, the core elements, and how my seizures connected me to another world. As I spoke, I could see the skepticism growing in their eyes, but I pressed on, determined to make them understand.

"I know it sounds crazy, but it's real. Every time I have a seizure, I find myself in Kenyzee's body on Three Astral.

I've seen things, felt things that are beyond explanation. It's not just dreams or hallucinations. It's another reality."

My father shook his head, his expression a mix of disbelief and frustration. "Tathastu, you've been through a lot. It's normal to have vivid dreams or even hallucinations after taking such strong medication. But you need to understand that it's all in your mind."

### *The Doctor's Diagnosis*

The door to my room opened, and Dr. Sharma, the psychiatrist, walked in. He had a kind face, but his eyes were serious as he looked at me and then at my family.

"I've been informed about what Tathastu has been experiencing," he said, taking a seat beside my bed. "And I believe we need to have a serious conversation about his mental health."

My heart sank as I listened to Dr. Sharma explain that my experiences were likely a result of a personality disorder. He spoke about dissociative identity disorder and how stress, trauma, and intense emotions could cause a person to create alternate realities in their mind as a coping mechanism.

"Tathastu, what you're experiencing feels real to you, and that makes it very challenging. But it's important to understand that these are constructs of your mind, ways your brain is trying to deal with stress and trauma. We need to work on grounding you in reality and helping you distinguish between what's real and what's not."

### *The Family's Reaction*

My mother started to cry softly, her tears falling onto the bed sheets. "Oh, Tathastu, I just want you to be okay. We'll do whatever it takes to help you. We'll get through this together."

My father nodded, his expression softening. "We love you, son. We're here for you, no matter what."

My sister squeezed my hand, her eyes filled with tears. "We're in this together, Tathastu. We'll help you get better."

Despite their words of support, I felt a deep sense of isolation. They couldn't understand what I had been through, what I had seen and felt. To them, it was a disorder, a figment of my imagination. But to me, it was real, more real than anything I had ever experienced on Earth.

### *The Reality of Three Astral*

As the days passed, I tried to follow the doctor's advice. I attended therapy sessions, took the prescribed medications, and made an effort to stay grounded in reality. But the memories of Three Astral were vivid and persistent, haunting my thoughts and dreams.

One day, as I sat in my room, I absentmindedly ran my fingers over the wooden desk beside my bed. To my astonishment, I felt a faint vibration, a whisper of connection. The wood seemed to pulse with a life of its own, responding to my touch.

"Hello?" I whispered, feeling a rush of excitement and fear.

The wood didn't reply, but the sensation was unmistakable. It was the same feeling I had experienced on Three Astral, the sense of being connected to the core elements, to the very fabric of another world.

### *The Final Understanding*

I realized then that, no matter what the doctors said, no matter how much my family worried, Three Astral was real to me. It wasn't just a disorder or a coping mechanism. It was a part of my reality, a part of who I was.

In the quiet moments, when I was alone with my thoughts, I could still feel the presence of the core elements, the echo of Lika's voice, and the weight of the responsibilities I had taken on in that other world. It was a truth I couldn't deny, even if no one else could understand it.

### *Mental Disorder or Reality*

One day, I was sitting near a tree, my mind a whirlwind of thoughts and uncertainties. The doctors' reassurances echoed in my mind, but doubt lingered like a shadow. Were they right? Or was Three Astral and the life I experienced there somehow real? The questions gnawed at me, leaving me restless and confused.

I took a deep breath and closed my eyes, seeking solace in the natural world around me. I focused intently, trying to connect with the plants and animals on Earth. To my amazement, I felt a subtle energy, a gentle pulsing that seemed to resonate with the life around me. It was faint at first, but as I concentrated harder, the connection grew stronger.

Tentatively, I reached out with my mind, asking the nearby birds to come to me. I wasn't sure if it would work, but I had to try. The air seemed to hum with anticipation, and then, one by one, the birds began to gather. First, a few fluttered down from the branches, then dozens more joined, until there were hundreds, and finally over a thousand birds surrounded me.

The sight was nothing short of miraculous. People nearby stopped in their tracks, their faces a mix of awe and disbelief. They whispered to one another, pointing at the spectacle unfolding before their eyes. It was as if time itself had paused, the world holding its breath.

I opened my eyes to see the sky darkened with the flurry of wings, the tree branches heavy with birds. The air was filled with the soft rustling of feathers and the occasional chirp, a symphony of nature responding to my call. My heart swelled with a mixture of wonder and exhilaration, the doubts that had plagued me momentarily forgotten.

After witnessing the incredible scene, Dr. Sharma, his face pale with shock, stammered, "He... he might be telling the truth about everything."

# END

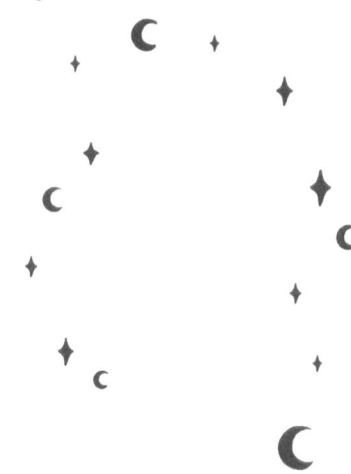

# Middle Part of the Book

## Chapter - 1
# The Origin

The Big Bang Theory is one of the most fundamental concepts in cosmology, explaining the origin and evolution of the universe. The theory proposes that the universe began as a singularity approximately 13.8 billion years ago. A singularity is a point in space-time where density and gravitational forces are infinite, and the laws of physics as we know them cease to operate. From this infinitesimally small point, the universe began to expand in an event known as the Big Bang.

The Big Bang was not an explosion in the traditional sense, but rather a rapid expansion of space itself. Imagine a balloon being inflated; every point on the surface moves away from every other point as the balloon expands. Similarly, in the Big Bang, space itself expanded, carrying galaxies with it, causing them to move away from each other.

## *The Concept of Parallel Universes*

The concept of parallel universes, often referred to as the multiverse, is one of the most fascinating and mind-bending ideas in modern physics. It suggests that our universe is not the only one that exists; rather, there are potentially an infinite number of universes existing simultaneously, each with its own distinct properties and laws of physics. This notion significantly broadens our understanding of the cosmos and challenges the idea that our universe is unique.

The Big Bang Theory, which explains the origin of our universe, can be extended to include the birth of multiple universes. According to this extended theory, the initial singularity that led to the Big Bang did not create just one universe, but rather a vast number of universes. This idea is supported by several theoretical frameworks in cosmology and quantum mechanics.

One of the primary theories supporting the existence of parallel universes is the concept of cosmic inflation. Proposed by physicist Alan Guth in the early 1980s, cosmic inflation suggests that the universe underwent an exponential expansion in the first fractions of a second after the Big Bang. During this period, the universe expanded much faster than the speed of light, smoothing out any irregularities and setting the stage for the formation of galaxies and large-scale structures.

For example, if a particle can spin either up or down, the MWI posits that the universe splits into two branches: one where the particle spins up and another where it spins down. This process occurs continuously, leading to an ever-growing number of parallel universes. Each universe represents a different possible outcome of every quantum event, resulting in a vast, possibly infinite, multiverse.

## Chapter - 2
# Formation of Earth

**The Solar Nebula and the Birth of the Sun**

Around 4.6 billion years ago, a massive molecular cloud, known as the solar nebula, existed in one of the spiral arms of the Milky Way galaxy. This cloud was composed primarily of hydrogen and helium, with traces of heavier elements that had been produced in previous generations of stars. The solar nebula was part of a much larger interstellar cloud complex, remnants of ancient supernovae that had enriched the interstellar medium with heavy elements.

A nearby supernova explosion likely triggered the collapse of a region within this solar nebula. The shockwave from the supernova compressed the gas and dust, causing it to clump together and form denser regions. As these regions continued to collapse under their own gravity, they formed a rotating disk of gas and dust known as a protoplanetary disk.

At the center of this disk, the material coalesced to form a protostar, which would eventually become our Sun. As the protostar grew in mass, it began to heat up, igniting nuclear fusion in its core. This process released an enormous amount of energy, causing the protostar to shine brightly and enter the T-Tauri phase, a stage in stellar development characterized by strong stellar winds and magnetic activity.

These stellar winds blew away much of the remaining gas and dust from the inner regions of the protoplanetary disk, leaving behind the solid materials that would form the planets, moons, and other bodies of the Solar System.

## Formation of the Planets

The formation of planets began with the process of accretion, where small particles of dust and ice collided and stuck together to form larger clumps called planetesimals. These planetesimals, which ranged in size from small rocks to objects hundreds of kilometers in diameter, continued to collide and merge, gradually building up into protoplanets.

In the inner regions of the protoplanetary disk, where temperatures were higher, planetesimals were primarily composed of rocky and metallic materials. This led to the formation of the terrestrial planets, including Mercury, Venus, Earth, and Mars. These planets are characterized by their solid, rocky surfaces and relatively high densities.

In the outer regions of the disk, where temperatures were lower, planetesimals contained a higher proportion of ices and gases. This resulted in the formation of the gas giants Jupiter and Saturn, as well as the ice giants Uranus and Neptune. These planets have thick atmospheres composed mainly of hydrogen, helium, and other volatile compounds, and they possess extensive systems of moons and rings.

# Evolution of Earth

Earth formed in the inner region of the protoplanetary disk, where rocky planetesimals were abundant. Over tens of millions of years, these planetesimals collided and merged, growing larger and larger through the process of accretion. As the protoplanet continued to accumulate mass, its gravity increased, allowing it to attract even more material.

During this time, Earth experienced intense heating due to the energy released from collisions, the decay of radioactive elements, and the gravitational compression of the growing planet. This heating caused the early Earth to become partially molten, allowing heavier materials, such as iron and nickel, to sink towards the center and form the core, while lighter materials, such as silicates, rose to the surface to form the mantle and crust. This differentiation process resulted in a layered structure, with a dense metallic core, a semi-solid mantle, and a solid outer crust.

## *Other Parallel Universe and the Creation of Three Core Elements*

While the Big Bang in our universe led to the formation of stars, galaxies, and planets, including Earth, the same event in a parallel universe resulted in a unique outcome. In this parallel universe, the Big Bang not only initiated the expansion of space but also gave birth to three fundamental core elements: Blue (Teal), Red (Ruby) and Green (Jade). These core elements, unlike the particles in our universe, began their journey traveling in the same direction through the vast expanse of their universe.

## The Parallel Universe's Big Bang

Just as the Big Bang in our universe marked the beginning of time and space, the parallel universe's Big Bang was an explosive event that set everything in motion. The initial conditions of this parallel universe were slightly different from our own, leading to the creation of the three core elements right from the start. The immense energy and rapid expansion created a primordial soup from which these core elements emerged.

## Formation of the Three Core Elements

In this parallel universe, the Big Bang's explosive energy caused the formation of three distinct core elements. These elements were not just random particles but fundamental building blocks with unique properties. From the very first moments after the Big Bang, the Blue, Red, and Green core elements were created amidst the rapidly expanding and cooling universe.

The creation of these core elements can be attributed to the unique conditions present during the Big Bang in this parallel universe. The initial singularity contained a different set of physical laws and constants, leading to the emergence of these three core elements instead of the familiar hydrogen and helium that dominated our universe's early moments.

## The Directional Movement

Unlike the particles in our universe, which dispersed in all directions, the three core elements in this parallel universe began traveling in a single direction. This coordinated movement can be explained by the anisotropy present in the initial moments of the Big Bang. Anisotropy refers to the variation of physical properties in different directions, and in this parallel universe, it caused the core elements to move along a specific axis.

As the universe continued to expand, the Blue, Red, and Green core elements maintained their directional journey. This movement was not random but rather a result of the initial conditions set by the Big Bang. The directional travel of these core elements had significant implications for the evolution of their universe.

## Chapter – 3
# The Formation of Three Astral Planet

### *The Interstellar Cataclysm*

Approximately 16 billion years ago, a massive star named R136a1 in our universe (the universe where the Earth is located) reached the end of its life cycle. R136a1, located in the Large Magellanic Cloud, was one of the largest stars ever known, about 2,616 times more massive than our Sun. When R136a1 exhausted its nuclear fuel, it collapsed under its own gravity and exploded in a spectacular supernova, releasing an immense amount of energy.

The supernova was so powerful that its shockwaves traveled through the fabric of space-time, not only impacting our universe but also affecting a neighboring parallel universe. One of neighboring parallel universe was home to three core elements—Blue, Red, and Green—that were traveling together in the same direction.

## *The Cosmic Shockwave*

The shockwaves from the R136a1 supernova crossed the boundary between our universe and the neighboring parallel universe, carrying remnants of the star's outer layers, including heavy elements and cosmic dust. When these shockwaves encountered the path of the three core elements in the parallel universe, they caused a significant disruption.

The immense energy from the supernova altered the paths of the Blue, Red, and Green core elements. Previously, these elements were moving in a straight line, but the shockwave forced them to change direction. This change set the core elements on a new course, heading toward each other rather than moving independently.

## *Convergence and Attraction*

As the three core elements—Blue, Red, and Green—altered their paths due to the shockwave from the supernova, they began to move closer together. The force exerted by the shockwave disrupted their previous

*Three Astral: Thought's Deception*

straight-line movement and directed them towards each other. This new trajectory caused the gravitational pull between the elements to increase as the distance between them decreased.

As they drew nearer, the gravitational attraction between the Blue, Red, and Green core elements intensified. This mutual attraction was a result of the gravitational forces each element exerted on the others. Eventually, their paths intersected, causing them to stop moving independently and begin influencing each other directly.

The convergence of these core elements led to the formation of a stable triangular arrangement. This triangular configuration was the natural result of their mutual gravitational forces balancing out. Each core element exerted an equal and opposite gravitational pull on the others, creating a stable equilibrium. The center of this triangle became a unique space, perfectly balanced by the forces exerted by the Blue, Red, and Green core elements. This space was special because the combined gravitational forces from the three elements created a region where their influences were evenly distributed.

## *The Birth of Three Astral*

Within the triangular formation of the Blue, Red, and Green core elements, the space between them began to attract cosmic dust and particles from the surrounding universe. These particles, which were remnants of the Big Bang, started to accumulate in the center of the triangle. The gravitational forces from the core elements acted as a sort of cosmic net, drawing in and trapping these particles.

As time passed, more and more dust and particles gathered in this central space. The continuous accumulation of material caused the particles to clump together, gradually forming larger and larger masses. These particles to stick together and grow in size.

Eventually, these accumulated masses became large enough to coalesce into a new celestial body. This new body, formed from the cosmic dust and particles, was heavily influenced by the presence of the three core elements. The combined gravitational forces and the unique properties of the Blue, Red, and Green elements provided the necessary conditions for this new celestial body to take shape.

The birth of this new planet, known as Three Astral, was a direct result of the interactions between the core elements and the cosmic material they attracted. The stability provided by the triangular arrangement of the core elements ensured that the newly formed planet had a balanced environment. The energy and connectivity supplied by the core elements influenced the planet's development, making it a unique and dynamic world within the parallel universe.

*Three Astral: Thought's Deception*

## Chapter - 4
# The Role of Core Elements

### *The Formation of Unique Regions*

The planet Three Astral is divided into three distinct regions, each uniquely shaped by one of the core elements: Red, Blue, and Green. These core elements not only define the geographical and climatic characteristics of each region but also grant the inhabitants the ability to harness and manipulate these elements to create what they need for their survival and prosperity.

**Red Core Region:** The Red Core region is characterized by its volcanic landscapes and extreme temperatures, driven by the fiery energy of the red core element. This region features molten lava fields, rugged mountains, and frequent volcanic eruptions. The heat from the red core fuels continuous geological activity, creating a dynamic and ever-changing environment. The inhabitants of this region, known as the Kaji, can harness the power of the red core element to control and manipulate fire. They use this ability to forge tools and weapons, build their homes, and power their industries. The mastery over fire also allows them to cook food, provide warmth, and engage in ceremonial rituals that are central to their culture.

**Blue Core Region:** The Blue Core region stands in stark contrast to the Red Core region, characterized by vast icy landscapes, including glaciers, frozen lakes, and snow-covered plains. The cooling and stabilizing energy of the blue core element shapes this region, creating a relatively predictable and balanced environment. The stability provided by the blue core is essential for life forms that thrive in cold and stable conditions. The inhabitants of this region, known as the Kori, possess the ability to harness and manipulate ice and water. They use this power to construct shelters from ice, manage their water resources, and create intricate ice sculptures. The Kori can also create ice barriers for defense, control the flow of rivers, and generate ice-based tools and weapons that are crucial for their daily lives.

**Green Core Region:** The Green Core region is the most fertile and biologically diverse area of Three Astral. Influenced by the life-giving energy of the green core element, this region is covered in dense forests, sprawling grasslands, and vibrant ecosystems. The green core promotes growth and connectivity, resulting in a rich and complex web of life forms interconnected through various symbiotic relationships. The inhabitants of this region, known as the Midori, can harness the power of the green core element to influence plant growth and communicate with flora. They use this ability to cultivate crops, heal the land, and maintain the health of their environment. The Midori can grow medicinal plants, construct buildings from living trees, and create gardens that sustain their communities. Their deep connection to the green core allows them to live sustainably and in harmony with nature.

# Evolution of Life on Three Astral

## *The Birth of Microbial Life*

The formation of Three Astral was just the beginning. The planet, now rich with elemental energies from the red, blue, and green cores, set the stage for an extraordinary process: the evolution of life. Initially, life on Three Astral began with the emergence of simple, single-celled organisms. These microorganisms, analogous to Earth's prokaryotes, thrived in the nutrient-rich waters created by the blue core. Unlike Earth, however, the presence of the core elements meant that these early life forms were influenced by powerful elemental energies from the outset.

The microbial life on Three Astral quickly diversified. Some microorganisms adapted to the fiery environments shaped by the red core, developing heat-resistant enzymes and proteins that allowed them to survive and thrive in volcanic regions. Others specialized in the cold, icy habitats influenced by the blue core, evolving antifreeze proteins to prevent ice crystal formation within their cells. The green core nurtured a third group of microorganisms that excelled in photosynthesis, harnessing the core's life-giving energy to produce organic compounds from light.

These early adaptations laid the groundwork for a diverse microbial ecosystem. Microbes formed the base of the food web, creating a foundation upon which more complex life forms could evolve. Their metabolic activities also played a crucial role in shaping the planet's environment, contributing to the cycling of essential elements like carbon, nitrogen, and sulfur.

The transition from single-celled to multicellular life was a monumental leap in the evolution of life on Three Astral. This transition allowed for greater complexity and specialization, as cells within multicellular organisms could differentiate and perform distinct functions. The first multicellular organisms were simple colonies of cells that cooperated for mutual benefit, but over time, these colonies evolved into more complex and integrated forms.

The red, blue, and green cores continued to influence the evolution of life. The fiery regions dominated by the red core gave rise to organisms with robust, heat-resistant structures. These organisms developed tough exoskeletons and efficient respiratory systems to cope with the harsh conditions. In contrast, the icy environments shaped by the blue core favored the evolution of organisms with insulating layers of fat and specialized heat-generating tissues. The fertile regions influenced by the green core saw the emergence of organisms with extensive root systems and complex vascular structures, allowing them to absorb and transport nutrients efficiently.

The rise of multicellular life led to the development of the first complex ecosystems. Predatory and prey relationships emerged, driving evolutionary arms races and fostering diversity. Symbiotic relationships also became more common, with organisms forming mutually beneficial partnerships to enhance their survival and reproduction.

## Chapter - 5
# The Elemental Harmonizers

*Secret Power - The Elemental Harmonizers*

In addition to the general population, there are individuals on Three Astral who possess a unique ability to harmonize with the core elements. These rare individuals, known as Elemental Harmonizers, can match their frequency with that of the core elements, allowing them to wield their power with extraordinary precision and strength. Among these harmonizers are three exceptional beings, each representing their respective regions: a Kaji, a Kori, and a Midori.

**Kaji Harmonizer:** The Kaji Harmonizer, known as Riko, has an unparalleled mastery over fire. By harmonizing with the red core, Riko can manipulate fire in ways that surpass ordinary Kaji abilities. Riko can create massive firestorms, melt through the toughest metals, and even control the temperature of flames with fine precision. This power is not just about destruction; Riko can also use fire for healing purposes, cauterizing wounds and purifying water.

**Kori Harmonizer:** The Kori Harmonizer, named Airi, is a master of ice and water. By aligning with the blue core's frequency, Airi can summon blizzards, create intricate ice structures in an instant, and manipulate water at a molecular level. Airi's abilities include controlling the flow of rivers, creating ice barriers for protection, and even freezing enemies in their tracks. Additionally, Airi can use ice to preserve and heal, slowing down biological processes to extend life and prevent decay.

**Midori Harmonizer:** The Midori Harmonizer, called Sora, has an extraordinary connection to plant life and the green core. Sora can accelerate plant growth, communicate with flora, and heal the land. By matching the green core's frequency, Sora can create vast forests from barren land, summon vines and roots to defend against threats, and even rejuvenate dying ecosystems. Sora's power extends to creating potent herbal remedies and enhancing crop yields to sustain their community.

These Elemental Harmonizers play a crucial role in their societies, serving as guardians, healers, and leaders. Their ability to harmonize with the core elements allows them to maintain balance and peace on Three Astral, protecting their world from both internal and external threats. Their existence is a testament to the deep connection between the inhabitants of Three Astral and the elemental forces that shape their world.

## Chapter - 6
# The Threat of Dark Matter

### *The Shifting Blue Core*

The planet Three Astral, with its unique and harmonious environment shaped by the Red, Blue, and Green core elements, faced a new and unexpected threat. Over time, the Blue core element, which provided stability and cooling to one of the planet's regions, began to shift slightly away from the other two core elements. This subtle yet significant movement created a spatial imbalance, which had far-reaching consequences for the planet.

The Blue core element's shift was not immediately noticeable, but its effects gradually became apparent. The core, now farther from the Red and Green elements, left a void that allowed a mysterious and malevolent force to enter the space between them. This force was known as dark matter.

### *The Infiltration of Dark Matter*

Dark matter, an elusive and enigmatic substance, began to seep into the space created by the shifting Blue core. Unlike the life-giving energies of the core elements, dark matter possessed a destructive nature. It had the potential to decompose any material it came into contact with, breaking down the molecular structure of both organic and inorganic matter.

As dark matter infiltrated Three Astral, it spread insidiously through the regions, starting with the area around the Blue core. The inhabitants of Three Astral soon began to notice the effects of this malevolent substance. Structures began to deteriorate, plants withered, and even the ground itself seemed to lose its stability. The once thriving and vibrant environment of Three Astral was now under threat.

## *The Effects on the Inhabitants*

The presence of dark matter had a profound impact on the inhabitants of Three Astral. The Kori, who lived closest to the Blue core, were the first to feel its effects. Their ice structures began to melt and crumble, and their once stable environment became increasingly unpredictable. The Kori, known for their balance and tranquility, found themselves struggling to maintain their way of life in the face of this new threat.

The Midori, whose region was rich with plant life and biodiversity, saw their crops and forests begin to wither. The Green core's energy, while still powerful, could not fully counteract the decomposing force of dark matter. The Midori's deep connection to nature made them acutely aware of the ecological imbalance that dark matter was causing, and they worked tirelessly to find ways to protect their environment.

The Kaji, although initially less affected, began to notice the deterioration of their volcanic structures and geothermal energy sources. The Red core's fire could not easily combat the pervasive and insidious nature of dark matter. The Kaji, known for their strength and resilience, faced a new kind of challenge that required not just brute force, but ingenuity and cooperation.

## *The Growing Threat*

As dark matter continued to spread, it became clear that it posed a significant threat to the very existence of Three Astral. The core elements, while powerful, were not immune to the effects of dark matter. The delicate balance that had allowed the planet to thrive was now at risk, and the inhabitants faced the possibility of their world being consumed by this malevolent force.

Dark matter's ability to decompose and destabilize made it unlike any threat the inhabitants had faced before. Traditional methods of defense and protection were ineffective against it. The Elemental Harmonizers, Riko, Airi, and Sora, recognized the severity of the situation and began to explore new ways to combat this pervasive threat.

## Chapter – 7
# Solution to Tackle Dark Matter

### *Nitya - The Bright Mind of the Red Region*

In the heart of the fiery Red Core region, there lived an exceptional individual named Nitya. Renowned as the most intelligent being on Three Astral, Nitya dedicated her life to understanding the mysteries of the universe and finding solutions to the planet's most pressing problems. With a keen mind and an insatiable curiosity, she had become a leading figure in the scientific community of the Kaji.

When dark matter began infiltrating Three Astral, causing widespread destruction and destabilization, Nitya knew that this was a challenge unlike any On it should be off, other. She immersed herself in studying dark matter, determined to uncover its secrets and find a way to protect her world.

### *Experiments and Discoveries*

Nitya set up a laboratory in the volcanic caves of the Red Core region, using the heat and energy from the geothermal vents to power her experiments. She conducted numerous tests to understand the properties of dark matter, its behavior, and its interaction with different materials and energies.

One of her experiments involved isolating dark matter samples and exposing them to extreme heat, attempting to burn it away with the intense flames generated by the Red Core's energy. While the dark matter appeared to be temporarily suppressed by the fire, it always returned, proving resistant to complete destruction.

Another experiment focused on using electromagnetic fields to contain and neutralize dark matter. Nitya created powerful magnetic barriers, hoping to trap dark matter and render it inert. However, she found that dark matter could permeate even the strongest electromagnetic fields, slipping through and continuing its destructive course.

Through her relentless experimentation, Nitya concluded that dark matter could not be destroyed by conventional means. Its properties were unlike anything she had encountered before, capable of decomposing matter at a molecular level without being affected by typical physical or energetic forces.

### *Tracing the Origin of the Problem*

Undeterred by the challenges, Nitya shifted her focus to understanding the origin of the dark matter infiltration. She began by studying the recent changes in the alignment of the core elements. Through her research, Nitya discovered that the Blue core element had shifted away from the Red and Green cores, creating a spatial imbalance that allowed dark matter to enter Three Astral.

Nitya realized that restoring the original balance of the core elements was crucial to preventing further dark matter infiltration. She hypothesized that if the Blue core could be moved back to its original position, the spatial void allowing dark matter to enter would be closed, thus protecting the planet.

## *The Potential of the Elemental Harmonizers*

Nitya knew that the Elemental Harmonizers—Riko, Airi, and Sora—had unique abilities to connect with their respective core elements. However, each Harmonizer could only connect with one core element at a time. To move the Blue core back to its original position, Nitya theorized that a being capable of harmonizing with all three core elements simultaneously was needed.

This being would need to possess a perfect balance of the frequencies of the Red, Blue, and Green cores. Such an individual could manipulate the energies of all three cores, coordinating their movements and restoring the balance that had been disrupted.

## *Creating Kenyzee*

To achieve this, Nitya proposed creating a new being, Kenyzee, who would have the combined DNA and abilities of the Kaji, Kori, and Midori. This being would be designed to harmonize with all three core elements, drawing on the strengths and traits of each species.

Working with geneticists and engineers from all three regions, Nitya led the project to develop Kenyzee. They extracted DNA from the most powerful individuals of the Kaji, Kori, and Midori, and combined these genetic materials in a sophisticated bioengineering process. Kenyzee's body was carefully crafted to withstand the immense energies of the core elements and to be capable of achieving perfect elemental harmony.

Despite their best efforts, the team faced a significant challenge: Kenyzee, though physically perfect, was not alive. The complex genetic fusion required more than just biological material; it needed a spark of life to bring Kenyzee to consciousness.

## *The Theory of Frequency Resonance*

Nitya pondered this problem deeply and developed a new theory. She proposed that Kenyzee could be brought to life through a process called frequency resonance. According to her theory, every living being has a unique frequency, and Kenyzee required a specific frequency to match his genetic and elemental composition to activate his life force.

Nitya believed that if someone could match their frequency with Kenyzee's perfectly, they could transfer their life energy to him, effectively bringing him to life. This process would require a person with extraordinary harmony and balance within themselves, someone who could resonate with all three core elements.

The Elemental Harmonizers—Riko, Airi, and Sora—were identified as the best candidates for this task. They already had a deep connection with their respective core elements, and their combined efforts could create the perfect frequency needed to awaken Kenyzee.

The three Harmonizers underwent rigorous training to synchronize their energies and achieve the precise frequency required. They meditated, practiced elemental control, and worked closely with Nitya to fine-tune their abilities. The process was arduous, requiring immense concentration and cooperation.

Finally, the day arrived when they were ready to attempt the resonance. Riko, Airi, and Sora stood around Kenyzee, channeling their energies and focusing on achieving perfect harmony. As their frequencies aligned, a radiant light enveloped Kenyzee, and the dormant being began to stir. However, despite their best efforts and the apparent signs of success, Kenyzee did not come to life. The light faded, and the hope that had filled the room dissipated into silence.

Nitya and the Harmonizers were faced with the stark reality that, despite all their efforts and ingenuity, they could not bring Kenyzee to life. The solution to tackling dark matter remained elusive, and the challenge of protecting Three Astral from this destructive force continued to loom large

---

## *Turn To Chapter 1: Left Hand Side (Page no. 2)*

---

*Three Astral: Thought's Deception*

# Right Side/Three Astral-Based Chapters

# Chapter – 1
# Arrival on Three Astral

### *The Awakening*

As I opened my eyes, the first thing I saw was the upper side of a room unlike any I had ever seen on Earth. The ceiling was not a solid, inert surface but seemed to be made of a living substance, pulsating gently with a soft, bioluminescent glow. The light it emitted was soothing, casting the room in a serene, ethereal glow. The colors shifted slowly, blending from one hue to another, creating an otherworldly atmosphere.

I blinked several times, trying to clear my vision and make sense of what I was seeing. The room was filled with strange shapes and objects, none of which resembled anything I had seen before. The walls appeared to be alive, covered in a texture that looked like a cross between plant tissue and animal hide. They undulated slightly, as if breathing.

My heart pounded in my chest as I took in my surroundings. I felt a strange mixture of fear and curiosity. This place was alien, yet there was something strangely familiar about it, as if I had seen it in a dream. I struggled to sit up, my body feeling unusually light and agile. As I moved, I became aware of a new sensation, a connection to my surroundings that I had never experienced before.

The floor beneath me felt warm and organic, not like the cold, hard surfaces I was used to. It had a slight give to it, almost like stepping on a dense, living mat. As I pushed myself up, I noticed the texture of the floor seemed to ripple under my touch, responding to my movements. This entire environment was pulsating with life, a concept that was both mesmerizing and terrifying.

I took a deep breath, trying to calm the rapid beating of my heart. The air was fragrant, filled with unfamiliar yet pleasant scents that seemed to enhance my senses. Every breath I took felt more profound, more connected to the world around me. My ears picked up faint, harmonious sounds, a melody created by the natural rhythms of this strange place.

### *The New Body*

I looked down at my hands and gasped. They were not my hands. The skin was a smooth, shimmering blue, with intricate patterns that glowed faintly in the dim light. My fingers were longer and more slender than I remembered, and they moved with a grace and precision that was alien to me. The patterns on my skin seemed to shift and change with my movements, reflecting the ambient light in a way that was almost hypnotic.

I quickly examined the rest of my body. I was taller and more slender, my limbs longer and more flexible. My skin was covered in the same shimmering blue hue, the patterns swirling and shifting as I moved. I felt a strange sense of power and vitality coursing through me, a connection to the world around me that was both exhilarating and overwhelming.

I touched my face, feeling the smooth, cool surface of my new skin. My hair was different too, longer and finer, and it seemed to move slightly on its own, responding to the ambient currents in the air. I felt a strange mix of fear and awe as I realized that I was inhabiting a completely different body, one that was not my own.

My movements felt fluid and effortless, as if my body were perfectly attuned to this environment. There was an elegance to the way my limbs moved, a natural grace that felt entirely foreign yet oddly comfortable. I flexed my fingers, marveling at the range of motion and the delicate, precise control I had over each movement.

I glanced into a reflective surface on the wall, catching sight of my face. It was a face that was both mine and not mine, familiar yet entirely new. My eyes were larger and more luminous, with a depth and intensity that seemed to see beyond the physical. My hair flowed around my head like a halo, shimmering with an inner light. The sight of my reflection was both disconcerting and fascinating, a reminder of the profound transformation I had undergone.

## *The Alien Environment*

Slowly, I stood up, taking in more of my surroundings. The room was filled with strange, organic-looking furniture and objects. There was a bed made of woven plant fibers that seemed to grow directly out of the floor, a table formed from a living, pulsating material, and shelves that sprouted from the walls like branches.

The air was filled with a faint, sweet fragrance, and I could hear the soft hum of what sounded like distant machinery, though it seemed to be coming from the walls themselves. Everything in this place felt alive, connected in a way that was both beautiful and disconcerting.

I walked to a nearby window and looked outside. The landscape that greeted me was unlike anything I had ever seen. The sky was a deep, rich blue, dotted with unfamiliar constellations. The ground below was covered in lush, vibrant vegetation, with trees and plants that glowed softly in the twilight. In the distance, I could see towering structures that seemed to grow out of the planet surface, their surfaces shimmering with the same bioluminescent glow as everything else.

The sight outside the window was breathtaking. The landscape was a riot of colors, with plants and trees displaying hues I had never seen before. Some of the trees had leaves that glowed with a soft, internal light, casting gentle illumination on the ground below. Flowers of incredible size and complexity bloomed in vibrant colors, their petals shimmering in the breeze.

I could see creatures moving among the foliage, their forms fluid and graceful. They moved with a purpose, interacting with the environment in ways that suggested a deep symbiosis. Birds with iridescent feathers flitted between the trees, their calls creating a symphony of sounds that filled the air. The ground was covered in a thick, carpet-like moss that seemed to pulse with life, creating a living tapestry that stretched as far as the eye could see.

## *Coming to Terms*

As I stood by the window, trying to process everything I was seeing, a wave of emotions washed over me. Fear, awe, curiosity, and a strange sense of peace all mingled together. I felt a deep connection to this place, as if I were meant to be here, despite its alien nature. The fear began to ebb, replaced by a growing sense of wonder.

I turned away from the window and took a deep breath, trying to steady my nerves. The room, with its living walls and organic furniture, seemed to pulse with energy. I felt a strange connection to everything around me, as if the very air I was breathing was alive and aware.

The environment was overwhelming, every aspect of it designed to engage my senses in new and profound ways. I walked around the room, touching the walls, feeling the subtle vibrations that seemed to pass through them. Each object I touched responded to my presence, shifting and changing in subtle ways as if acknowledging my existence.

I sat down on the bed, feeling its warmth and gentle support. The material seemed to mold itself to my body, providing perfect comfort. I closed my eyes, trying to make sense of my new reality. The confusion was still there, but it was tempered by a sense of acceptance. This was my new world, my new body, and I had to come to terms with it.

I knew that I was in a place far beyond anything I had ever imagined, and I felt a mixture of fear and anticipation. There was so much to understand, so much to learn about this incredible world and my place in it. The journey ahead was uncertain, and I was filled with questions, but for now, I simply tried to absorb the reality of my new existence.

# Chapter - 2
# Hijoka and?

### *The Confusion*

As I continued to take in the strange surroundings of my new room, a deep sense of confusion and disorientation washed over me. Every detail of this place was so different from anything I had ever known. My mind struggled to make sense of the living walls, the pulsating light, and the unfamiliar scents. I felt an urgent need to understand where I was and what had happened to me.

I looked around, searching for something familiar. My eyes landed on what I assumed was a mirror, but it was too far to see my reflection clearly. I needed to see myself, to confirm what my mind was struggling to accept. As I moved towards the mirror, a deep, commanding voice echoed through the room.

"Do not be alarmed," the voice said. It was strong, yet reassuring. I turned quickly, my new reflexes sharp and immediate. Standing in the doorway was a tall, muscular figure with a deep red hue to his skin and patterns that seemed to pulse with energy. His hair was dark and wild, and his eyes glowed with a fierce intensity.

The figure's presence was both intimidating and calming. There was an aura of authority about him, but also a sense of protection. My heart raced as I tried to process his appearance and the significance of his words. I took a tentative step back, my mind racing with questions and uncertainties.

"Who are you?" I managed to ask, my voice trembling slightly.

"My name is Hijoka," he replied, his tone firm yet gentle. "You have undergone a significant transformation, and it is essential that you take things slowly. Do not be afraid; you are safe here."

### *The Living Bed*

Before I could react further, the bed I had been lying on began to shift and transform. I stepped back in shock as the woven plant fibers that had formed the bed reconfigured themselves into a humanoid shape. The figure stood before me, its surface shimmering with the same bioluminescent glow as the walls and furniture.

"Do not be afraid," the being said, its voice calm and soothing. "I am not merely a bed. I am your personal assistant, here to help you adapt to your new environment."

I stared at the being, trying to process this new development. "Who are you? What is this place? What has happened to me?" My questions tumbled out, driven by a mix of fear and curiosity.

"My name is Hijoka," the red-skinned figure said again, stepping forward. "And this," he gestured to the living bed, "is your personal assistant. You have undergone a significant transformation, and it is essential that you take things slowly."

The assistant nodded, its form shimmering with life. "Yes, you have just woken up for the first time. Your body and mind need time to adjust. Please, take it patiently. I will explain everything in due course."

"But I need to understand," I insisted. "I need to see myself, to know where I am."

The assistant's form shimmered and began to change again. This time, it transformed into a large, full-length mirror. "Very well," it said. "Look at your reflection, and I will answer your questions as best as I can."

## *The Personal Assistant*

I approached the mirror, my heart pounding with a mix of fear and anticipation. The reflection that greeted me was both familiar and utterly alien. The smooth, shimmering blue skin, the intricate patterns that glowed faintly, the long, slender fingers – all these features were mine, yet not mine. My eyes were larger and more luminous, with a depth and intensity that seemed to peer into my very soul. My hair flowed around my head like a halo, shimmering with an inner light.

The mirror reflected a figure that was both strange and mesmerizing. My new form was tall and elegant, with a grace that seemed almost otherworldly. The patterns on my skin shifted and changed with my movements, creating a mesmerizing display of light and color. My fingers moved with a delicate precision, each motion controlled and deliberate.

I ran my fingers over my face, feeling the smooth, cool surface of my new skin. The reality of my transformation was starting to sink in, but it was overwhelming. My body felt powerful and vital, yet completely foreign. The connection I felt to the world around me was unlike anything I had ever experienced.

The assistant's voice broke the silence. "You are now in a body designed for life on Three Astral. This world is unique, where the boundaries between the physical and the living are blurred. The patterns on your skin are a form of communication, a way to interact with the environment around you. Your new body is stronger, more agile, and more attuned to the energies of this world."

### *Understanding My New Body*

The assistant continued, "Your senses are heightened, and you will find that you can perceive things beyond the normal range of any living being's experience. This is necessary for you to fulfill your role here."

I continued to examine my reflection, taking in every detail of my new form. My eyes, now larger and more luminous, seemed to hold a depth of knowledge and understanding that was both intriguing and disconcerting. My hair, flowing around my head like a halo, shimmered with an inner light that pulsed gently with my heartbeat.

My movements felt fluid and effortless, as if my body were perfectly attuned to this environment. There was an elegance to the way my limbs moved, a natural grace that felt entirely foreign yet oddly comfortable. I flexed my fingers, marveling at the range of motion and the delicate, precise control I had over each movement.

I glanced into the reflective surface again, catching sight of my face. It was a face that was both mine and not mine, familiar yet entirely new. My eyes were larger and more luminous, with a depth and intensity that seemed to see beyond the physical. My hair flowed around my head like a halo, shimmering with an inner light. The sight of my reflection was both disconcerting and fascinating, a reminder of the profound transformation I had undergone.

### *The First Encounter*

Just as I was beginning to come to terms with my reflection, a new voice echoed through the room. "Hi, Kenyzee."

I turned towards the sound, my heart skipping a beat. The voice was soft and melodic, filled with warmth and familiarity. It resonated with a depth that seemed to touch something deep within me, a name that felt both strange and deeply personal.

"Kenyzee?" I repeated, my voice barely a whisper.

I turned to Hijoka, my mind racing with questions. "Who is Kenyzee?"

Hijoka's expression softened. "You are Kenyzee," he said gently. "Be patient. She is coming."

"She? Who is coming? And why does this voice feel so familiar?" I asked, confusion and curiosity swirling within me.

"All will be explained in time," Hijoka replied. "For now, you need to rest. This is the first time you have woken up. Take it patiently."

As Hijoka spoke, the living assistant transformed back into its original form, its surface shimmering with life. I lay back down, my mind a whirlwind of thoughts and emotions. The name Kenyzee echoed in my mind

## Chapter - 3
# Meeting with Lika

### *The First Greeting*

The room remained bathed in its soft, bioluminescent glow, casting gentle hues of light that shifted and danced along the living walls. As I lay there, still reeling from the confusion and strangeness of my new existence, a soft, melodic voice reached my ears. "Hi, Kenyzee," it said, filled with warmth and familiarity.

I turned towards the sound, my heart skipping a beat. Standing in the doorway was the most beautiful being I had ever seen. She was tall and slender, her skin a shimmering blue adorned with intricate patterns that seemed to glow from within. Her hair flowed like liquid silver, cascading around her shoulders, and her eyes sparkled with a soft, inner light. Her presence was both calming and mesmerizing, and I couldn't help but feel a deep emotional connection to her voice and appearance.

Her clothing was unlike anything I had ever seen, made of a material that seemed to flow and change color with her movements, enhancing her ethereal beauty. The way she moved was graceful and fluid, as if she were gliding rather than walking. Every step she took seemed to resonate with the very fabric of the room, as if she were in perfect harmony with her surroundings.

As she approached, I felt a strange mixture of awe and comfort. There was something about her that made me feel safe, even amidst the confusion and uncertainty of my current situation. Her eyes met mine, and I saw a depth of understanding and empathy that made me feel seen in a way I had never experienced before.

## *An Emotional Encounter*

My emotions surged, a mix of awe, confusion, and a strange sense of recognition. It felt as if I had known her all my life, yet I was sure I had never seen her before. Her beauty was beyond anything I had ever encountered, ethereal and otherworldly, and it left me momentarily speechless.

She approached me with a gentle smile, her movements graceful and fluid. "How are you feeling, Kenyzee?" she asked, her voice soothing and kind. There was genuine concern in her eyes as she looked at me, and I felt a sense of comfort and safety in her presence.

I tried to find my voice, struggling to articulate the whirlwind of emotions swirling within me. "I... I don't know," I finally managed to say. "Everything feels so strange. Who are you? Why do I feel like I know you?"

Her smile widened slightly, and she reached out to touch my arm, her hand cool and reassuring. "It's natural to feel disoriented. You've been through a lot. My name is Lika, and I'm here to help you."

Her touch sent a calming wave through me, and I felt some of my tension ease. The kindness in her eyes and the warmth in her voice made me feel less alone in this strange new world. Despite the confusion, there was a part of me that instinctively trusted her.

### *Checking My Health*

Lika reached out and gently placed her hand on my forehead. Her touch was cool and calming, and I could feel a sense of energy flowing from her into me. "You've been through a lot," she said softly. "You have just woken up after a long time. Your body and mind need to recover."

I nodded, still trying to process everything. "Who am I? What happened to me?" I asked, my voice trembling with emotion. "Why do I feel like I know you?"

Lika's expression was one of understanding and empathy. "You are Kenyzee," she said. "Your memories are fragmented due to the accident, but don't worry. I am here to help you through this. For now, you need to rest."

As she spoke, she moved her hands over my body, her touch gentle and reassuring. She seemed to be checking my vital signs, though the method was unlike any medical procedure I had ever experienced. Her hands emitted a soft glow, and I felt a warm, soothing energy flow through me, easing my physical discomfort and calming my mind.

Her movements were precise and deliberate, and I could sense her deep knowledge and expertise. She seemed to be in tune with my body in a way that went beyond conventional medicine, her touch not only healing but also comforting. The fear and confusion that had gripped me began to subside, replaced by a growing sense of trust in this remarkable being.

## *Seeking Answers*

Despite her reassuring words, my mind was filled with questions. "But who am I really? Why do I feel like I know you? What is this place?" My voice grew more urgent with each question, the need for answers overwhelming my sense of patience.

Lika gently squeezed my hand, her eyes filled with compassion. "I understand how confusing this must be for you, Kenyzee. But you need to take things slowly. Your body and mind need time to heal. I promise you, we will talk about everything, but for now, please rest."

Her words were kind, but the lack of immediate answers only fueled my frustration and confusion. "Please, just tell me something," I pleaded. "I need to know."

Lika sighed softly, her expression gentle yet firm. "I know this is hard, but you must trust me. You have been through a significant trauma, and your memories will take time to return. For now, you need to focus on your recovery. Tomorrow, we will begin to answer all your questions."

She helped me lie back down, her touch soothing and comforting. "Rest now, Kenyzee. I am here to take care of you. Everything will be explained in due time."

I lay back on the bed, my mind still racing with questions. The soft glow of the room seemed to pulse gently, as if encouraging me to relax. Lika's presence by my side was a source of immense comfort, and despite my lingering confusion, I began to feel a sense of peace.

### *The Promise of Answers*

Lika stayed with me until I felt my eyelids grow heavy. Her soothing presence and gentle voice gradually eased my mind. "Don't worry about anything tonight," she said softly. "Just rest. Tomorrow is a new day, and we will face it together."

Her promise of answers gave me a glimmer of hope amidst the turmoil of my thoughts. I knew that there were many things I needed to understand, but for now, I had to trust her and focus on my recovery.

As I drifted off to sleep, her words echoed in my mind, bringing a sense of calm. The name Kenyzee, the feeling of familiarity with Lika, and the promise of answers tomorrow gave me the strength to let go of my immediate anxieties. I knew that I was not alone in this strange new world, and with Lika by my side, I felt a small measure of peace amidst the confusion.

### *Resting with Reassurance*

Lika's presence remained a comforting constant as I drifted towards sleep. The soft light of the room seemed to envelop me in a warm embrace, and I felt the stress in my body begin to melt away. The promise of answers, though delayed, provided a thread of hope that I clung to.

I lay there, replaying the events of the day in my mind. The transformation, the new body, the encounter with Hijoka, and now meeting Lika – it was all so overwhelming. Yet, there was a part of me that felt drawn to this new reality, a part that was eager to uncover the truth.

As I closed my eyes, the image of Lika's compassionate face remained with me. Her promise to explain everything tomorrow was a beacon of hope, and I found myself trusting her implicitly. Despite the uncertainty and confusion, I felt a growing sense of connection to this place and these people.

The soft, melodic hum of the room lulled me into a deeper state of relaxation. I could feel the living walls and furniture responding to my presence, as if they were attuned to my needs. The sensation was both comforting and surreal, a reminder that I was in a world far beyond my previous understanding.

As I finally succumbed to sleep, I felt a profound sense of anticipation for the day ahead. The journey was just beginning, and though the path was uncertain, I knew that with Lika's guidance, I would find the answers I sought. For now, I allowed myself to rest, knowing that I was in safe hands.

## Chapter – 4
# Journey to the Green Core Element

### *Awakening*

The morning light filtered into the room, casting a soft, ethereal glow over everything. I awoke feeling surprisingly refreshed, the confusion and anxiety from the previous day having receded somewhat. As I stretched and sat up, I saw Lika enter the room with a warm smile on her face.

"Good morning, Kenyzee," she greeted me. "How are you feeling today?"

"I feel... better," I replied, still marveling at the sound of my own voice, which seemed more resonant and clearer than before. "Thank you for staying with me last night."

Lika nodded; her eyes filled with kindness. "It was my pleasure. Today, we have much to discuss and many things to show you. Are you ready to learn more about who you are and where you come from?"

I nodded eagerly, the curiosity that had been burning within me reigniting. "Yes, please. I need to understand."

Lika's smile widened as she sat beside me, her presence comforting and reassuring. "You've come a long way, Kenyzee. Today, we'll begin to explore the depth of your own identity and the powers that come with it."

I took a deep breath, still trying to process everything that had happened. The room around me seemed to pulse with life, the walls gently glowing with an ever-shifting light. Every detail, from the bioluminescent plants to the organic furniture, spoke of a world that was as alive as I was. It was both awe-inspiring and overwhelming.

. The world of Three Astral was even more breathtaking in the daylight. The vibrant vegetation, the glowing trees, and the harmonious sounds of the wildlife created a scene of unparalleled beauty and tranquility.

Lika led me through the location, where I noticed other beings similar to us, each one radiating a sense of peace and unity. They smiled and greeted us as we passed, their expressions kind and welcoming. It was clear that this was a community that valued connection and harmony.

"Where are we going?" I asked, my curiosity piqued.

"We are going to visit the green core element," Lika explained. "It is the source of our strength and vitality. By connecting with it, you will gain a deeper understanding of your abilities and the role you are destined to play."

I nodded, eager to learn more. The path we took wound through lush forests and across serene meadows. Every step seemed to bring a new wonder into view. Strange, beautiful flowers bloomed along the path, their petals shimmering with an inner light. Birds with iridescent feathers flitted among the trees, their songs filling the air with a melodious symphony.

As we walked, Lika explained more about the Greenions. "We are a community deeply connected to the natural world. Our abilities allow us to foster growth and healing, not just within ourselves but in the environment around us. The green core element amplifies these abilities, making us integral to the balance and harmony of Three Astral."

She pointed out various plants and creatures along the way, explaining their unique properties and how they contributed to the ecosystem. "Every living being here is connected to the green core in some way. Our abilities enable us to communicate with these life forms, fostering a deep sense of unity and cooperation."

As we walked through the village, Lika pointed out a creature that caught my eye. "Look there," she said, gesturing towards a small, glowing animal perched on a branch. "That is a Lumifern."

The Lumifern was a small, fox-like creature with fur that glowed softly in shades of green and blue. Its eyes were large and intelligent, and its tail was bushy and shimmered with tiny lights, much like the bioluminescent plants around us. The creature seemed to be watching us with a curious expression, its ears twitching attentively.

"Lumiferns are closely connected to the green core element, just like you," Lika explained. "They have the ability to emit a healing light that can mend wounds and rejuvenate plants. Their presence is a sign of a healthy and thriving ecosystem. Greenions and Lumiferns share a special bond, often working together to maintain the balance of our environment."

I watched in fascination as the Lumifern leapt gracefully from the branch and landed lightly on the ground. It approached us cautiously, its glowing fur casting a soft light on the path. Lika knelt down and extended her hand, and the Lumifern nuzzled her fingers affectionately.

"These creatures are incredibly sensitive to the energies of the green core," Lika continued. "They can sense when the balance is disturbed and will often come to the aid of those in need. Their healing abilities are a reflection of the core's power, and their presence brings harmony to our world."

I listened intently, fascinated by the depth of knowledge and wisdom she shared. The connection between the Greenions and their environment was unlike anything I had ever seen. It was a relationship built on mutual respect and understanding, a harmonious balance that was both beautiful and profound.

The journey through the forest was a revelation in itself. I felt the energy of the green core element all around me, a vibrant pulse that connected every living thing. It was as if the very air was alive with the essence of growth and renewal, and I was becoming more attuned to it with each step.

As we continued our journey, the path began to ascend, leading us to higher ground. The forest thinned, giving way to a breathtaking vista of the surrounding landscape. I could see the entire expanse of Three Astral laid out before me – the lush forests, the shimmering lakes, and the distant mountains that seemed to touch the sky.

Lika paused for a moment, allowing me to take in the view. "This is your home now, Kenyzee," she said softly. "It is a world of wonder and beauty, but it is also a world that needs your strength and wisdom. The green core element is a part of you, and you are a part of it. Embrace this connection, and you will find your place here."

Her words resonated deeply within me. For the first time, I felt a true sense of belonging. The journey to the green core element was not just a physical one; it was a journey of discovery, a path that would lead me to understand my true self and the role I was meant to play in this incredible world.

As we resumed our walk, I felt a renewed sense of purpose. The path ahead was still unknown, but with Lika by my side and the green core element within reach, I knew that I was ready to face whatever challenges lay ahead.

### *The Journey Begins*

As we continued our walk, Lika guided me towards a structure that seemed to be made entirely of living plants. It was a beautiful blend of nature and architecture, with vines and flowers woven into the walls and roof. "This is where we will have our lunch," Lika explained.

Inside the structure, the atmosphere was serene and calming. A soft, green light filled the room, emanating from a series of crystals that hung from the ceiling like chandeliers. The light was warm and inviting, making the room feel both cozy and expansive.

"Lunch here is a bit different from what you might be used to," Lika said with a smile. "We connect directly to the green core element to nourish ourselves. It is a unique experience that strengthens our bond with the core and revitalizes our energy."

She led me to a comfortable seat, and as I settled in, I noticed thin, delicate strands of light descending from the crystals above. Lika guided me on how to connect these strands to my hair, explaining that they were conduits for the green core's energy.

"These strands will transmit the energy from the core directly into your body," she said. "It is a way for us to receive nourishment and strengthen our connection to the green core element."

As I connected the strands to my hair, I felt a gentle warmth spread through me. The energy was soothing and invigorating, filling me with a sense of vitality and well-being. It was unlike any meal I had ever experienced, a profound communion with the life force of Three Astral.

Lika watched me with a knowing smile. "It takes some getting used to, but you'll find that this method of nourishment is incredibly effective. It aligns us with the core's energy and helps us maintain our strength and resilience."

After our lunch, which left me feeling deeply refreshed and energized, we stepped out of the room and continued our journey. The fresh air hit my face, filled with the scents of blooming flowers. The world of Three Astral was even more breathtaking in the daylight. The vibrant vegetation, the glowing trees, and the harmonious sounds of the wildlife created a scene of unparalleled beauty and tranquility.

"We are going to visit the green core element," Lika explained as we walked. "It is the source of our strength and vitality. By connecting with it, you will gain a deeper understanding of your abilities and the role you are destined to play."

The path we took wound through lush forests and across serene meadows. Every step seemed to bring a new wonder into view. Strange, beautiful flowers bloomed along the path, their petals shimmering with an inner light. Birds with iridescent feathers flitted among the trees, their songs filling the air with a melodious symphony.

As we walked, Lika explained more about the Greenions. "We are a community deeply connected to the natural world. Our abilities allow us to foster growth and healing, not just within ourselves but in the environment around us. The green core element amplifies these abilities, making us integral to the balance and harmony of Three Astral."

She pointed out various plants and creatures along the way, explaining their unique properties and how they contributed to the ecosystem. "Every living being here is connected to the green core in some way. Our abilities enable us to communicate with these life forms, fostering a deep sense of unity and cooperation."

### *The Green Core Element*

After what felt like hours of walking through the mesmerizing landscape of Three Astral, we finally arrived at our destination. The green core element was housed in a grand, ancient structure that seemed to be made entirely of living plants. Vines and flowers covered the walls, and the entire structure pulsed with a gentle, green light.

"This is the heart of our power," Lika said, her voice filled with reverence. "The green core element is more than just a source of energy; it is a living, breathing entity that connects all Greenions."

We entered the structure, and I was immediately struck by the sense of peace and vitality that filled the air. The green core element itself was a large, glowing orb suspended in the center of the room, surrounded by intricate patterns of living vines and flowers. The light it emitted was soft yet powerful, creating a sense of warmth and tranquility.

Lika guided me to stand before the orb. "Place your hand on the core," she instructed. "Feel its energy and let it flow through you."

I reached out and touched the orb, and a surge of energy coursed through my body. It was a sensation unlike anything I had ever felt – warm, invigorating, and deeply soothing. As the energy flowed through me, I felt an extraordinary connection, as if my mind had linked with the minds of all other Greenions. It was as though I could feel their thoughts, emotions, and experiences merging with mine, creating a profound sense of unity and belonging.

The connection was so intense that I could see visions of Greenions across the region, each one turning their eyes a bright green in response to my touch. It was as if they were acknowledging the connection, sharing in this moment of unity. This visual confirmation of our bond filled me with an even greater sense of purpose.

Visions began to fill my mind. I saw the history of the Greenions, their struggles and triumphs, and their deep connection to the natural world. I saw how they used their abilities to heal the land and protect the balance of Three Astral. Each vision was accompanied by the sensation of countless minds intertwined with mine, sharing knowledge and wisdom.

I also saw glimpses of my own potential – the ways in which I could use my abilities to help others and contribute to the harmony of this world. The core's energy filled me with a sense of purpose and belonging that I had never felt before.

Lika watched me with a proud smile. "Do you understand now, Kenyzee? You are a part of something much larger than yourself. The green core element has chosen you for a reason, and it is up to you to discover that reason and fulfill your destiny."

I nodded, tears of awe and gratitude streaming down my face. "I think I do, Lika. Thank you for showing me this." But still I am in confusion

As I began to process the experience, Lika's expression grew serious. "There is something you need to understand about the green core element, Kenyzee. It is incredibly powerful and cannot be touched by just anyone. If anyone without the proper connection or potential tries to touch it, the core will destroy them. Only those who are chosen, like you, can safely interact with it."

I looked at her, wide-eyed. "So it's dangerous?"

Lika nodded. "Yes, but you are special, Kenyzee. You have the potential to share the power of the green core element. However, this power comes with great responsibility. You must learn to control and use it wisely. Your journey is just beginning, and there is much for you to learn." Meanwhile, in my mind I was thinking about what journey she is talking about.

I felt a mixture of awe and apprehension. The responsibility that came with my new abilities was immense, and I knew that I had a long path ahead of me. But with Lika's guidance, I felt ready to face whatever challenges lay ahead.

Lika continued to explain the significance of the green core element. "The green core is the essence of life and renewal on Three Astral. It is a powerful source of energy that sustains all living beings connected to it. As a Greenion, you are directly linked to this core, drawing strength and vitality from it."

She walked around the orb, her hand gently brushing the vines that surrounded it. "The green core element is also a guardian of balance. It ensures that the energies of life and growth are distributed evenly throughout our world. This balance is crucial for the survival and prosperity of all living beings on Three Astral."

As I listened to her, I felt a deep sense of reverence for the green core element. It was not just a source of power; it was a living entity that played a vital role in the harmony of our world. I understood that my connection to the core was both a gift and a responsibility, one that I had to embrace fully.

Lika then showed me a series of intricate patterns etched into the walls of the structure. "These patterns represent the history and teachings of the Greenions," she explained. "They tell the story of our people and our relationship with the green core element. By studying these patterns, you can learn more about our culture and the wisdom of our ancestors."

I examined the patterns closely, marveling at the detail and craftsmanship. Each symbol and line seemed to convey a deeper meaning, a piece of the puzzle that made up the rich tapestry of Greenion history. It was a humbling experience, and I felt a profound connection to the generations that had come before me.

Lika placed a hand on my shoulder, her expression warm and encouraging. "You have much to learn, Kenyzee, but I have no doubt that you will grow into your role. The green core element has chosen you for a reason, and you have the potential to achieve great things." I am so confused about why this Core element selected me, what Lika is talking about? What is the journey. However, I decided to listen everything what she is telling to me.

Her words filled me with a sense of purpose and determination. I knew that my journey was just beginning, but I was ready to embrace the challenges and responsibilities that lay ahead. With Lika by my side and the guidance of the green core element, I felt confident that I could fulfill my destiny.

As we prepared to leave the structure, Lika paused and looked back at the glowing orb. "Remember, Kenyzee, the green core element is a part of you, and you are a part of it. Embrace this connection and let it guide you on your path. The journey will not be easy, but with strength and wisdom, you will find your place in this world."

Her words echoed in my mind as we stepped outside into the vibrant world of Three Astral. The path ahead was uncertain, but with the power of the green core element and the support of my fellow Greenions,

## Chapter - 5
# Introduction to Greenions (Midori)

### *The Viewing Window*

After our profound experience with the green core element, Lika guided me to another part of the ancient structure. We entered a room that was dimly lit, with a large, transparent window embedded into one of the walls. The window was surrounded by intricate designs and symbols that seemed to pulse with energy.

"This is the Viewing Window," Lika explained. "It is one of our most advanced technologies, capable of showing the past and present of Three Astral. It will help you understand the history and abilities of the Greenions, particularly the Midori species."

The window's surface shimmered, and then transformed into a vivid, three-dimensional display. It was as if we were looking through a portal into another world. Scenes from the history of Three Astral began to unfold before my eyes, drawing me into a mesmerizing journey through time.

### *The Origins of the Midori*

Lika began to narrate the history of the Midori species. "The Midori are one of the three main species on Three Astral, deeply connected to the green core element. They are known for their exceptional abilities to foster growth and rejuvenation. Their connection to nature is unparalleled, and they play a crucial role in maintaining the balance of our world."

As she spoke, the window displayed images of lush forests, verdant fields, and towering trees. I saw Midori beings moving gracefully through these landscapes, their bodies glowing with a soft green light. They were nurturing the plants and animals, their touch bringing life and vitality to everything they encountered.

"The Midori are the guardians of the forests," Lika continued. "They have the ability to communicate with plants and animals, fostering a deep sense of harmony and cooperation. Their powers allow them to accelerate growth, heal injuries, and even revive dying ecosystems."

The window showed a Midori elder named Elarion, who was known for his wisdom and mastery of the green core element. Elarion was an ancient being, his body intertwined with vines and flowers. He moved with a calm and deliberate grace, his presence exuding a profound sense of peace.

"Elarion is one of our most revered elders," Lika explained. "He has lived for centuries, guiding the Midori with his knowledge and experience. His connection to the green core element is so strong that he can sense the slightest disturbance in the environment and take action to restore balance."

I watched in awe as the window displayed Elarion leading a group of Midori through the forest. His presence seemed to calm the entire area, the plants and animals responding to his energy with a sense of tranquility and order. He communicated with the creatures around him, understanding their needs and ensuring that they thrived under his care.

## *The Abilities of the Midori*

Lika continued to explain the unique abilities of the Midori species. "The Midori can harness the energy of the green core element to perform incredible feats. Their powers include accelerated healing, enhanced strength and agility, and the ability to manipulate plants and trees."

The window showed scenes of Midori warriors training in the forest, their movements fluid and precise. They were using their abilities to leap great distances, blend into their surroundings, and control the growth of plants to create barriers and traps.

"These warriors are trained to protect our world from threats," Lika said. "They are skilled in combat and can use their abilities to defend the forests and the creatures that live within them. The Midori are not only healers but also fierce protectors of the natural world."

One of the warriors, named Sylara, stood out in the display. She was a young and agile Midori, her body radiating with green energy. Sylara moved with incredible speed and precision, her connection to the green core element allowing her to anticipate and counter any attack.

"Sylara is one of our most promising young warriors," Lika said with a hint of pride. "She has a natural talent for using the green core element in combat. Her agility and strength are unmatched, and she is deeply committed to protecting our world."

Sylara's movements were almost hypnotic, her agility making her seem more like a part of the forest than a separate entity. She moved through the trees as if they were an extension of her own body, blending seamlessly into the foliage. I watched in awe as she demonstrated her abilities, leaping from tree to tree with incredible grace and speed.

The window then shifted to show Sylara in a sparring match with another warrior. The intensity of their training was palpable, each move calculated and executed with precision. Sylara's ability to manipulate the environment to her advantage was remarkable. She used vines to entangle her opponent and created barriers of foliage to protect herself.

### *The Role of the Midori in Society*

As the scenes continued to unfold, Lika explained the broader role of the Midori in Greenion society. "The Midori are not only warriors and healers but also teachers and leaders. They play a vital role in educating the younger generations about the importance of balance and harmony with nature."

The window showed a Midori school, where young Greenions were learning about the green core element and their connection to the natural world. Elarion was there, teaching the children with patience and wisdom. The young Greenions listened intently, their eyes wide with wonder as they absorbed the lessons.

"The Midori believe that knowledge and wisdom should be passed down through the generations," Lika said. "They teach the importance of respect for all living things and the responsibility that comes with their abilities. This education is crucial for maintaining the balance and harmony of our world."

Another figure appeared in the display, a Midori elder named Arannis. He was a scholar and a historian, dedicated to preserving the knowledge and history of the Greenions. Arannis spent his days documenting the stories and teachings of the elders, ensuring that the wisdom of the past would not be forgotten.

"Arannis is our greatest historian," Lika explained. "He has devoted his life to preserving our culture and history. His work ensures that the lessons of the past are remembered and that future generations can learn from them."

Arannis was a dignified figure, his presence exuding a quiet strength and determination. He moved slowly, with deliberate care, as he transcribed the ancient texts and recorded the stories of the elders. His dedication to preserving the knowledge of the Greenions was evident in every meticulous stroke of his pen.

I watched as Arannis guided a group of young Greenions through the archives. He showed them ancient manuscripts, each one a treasure trove of knowledge and wisdom. The young Greenions were captivated by his stories, their faces filled with curiosity and awe as they learned about their heritage.

Arannis's teachings extended beyond the written word. He often took his students into the forest, showing them the practical applications of their knowledge. They learned how to identify different plants and their uses, how to communicate with animals, and how to sense the energy of the green core element.

### *The Connection to the Green Core*

Finally, Lika spoke about the deep connection between the Midori and the green core element. "The Midori's abilities are directly linked to the green core. Their connection allows them to draw upon its energy and use it to heal, grow, and protect."

The window displayed a sacred ceremony, where Midori elders and warriors gathered around the green core element. They placed their hands on the orb, their bodies glowing with green light as they absorbed its energy. The scene was both awe-inspiring and humbling, a testament to the power of the green core and the unity of the Midori.

"This ceremony is a vital part of our culture," Lika explained. "It reinforces the bond between the Midori and the green core element. By connecting with the core, they renew their strength and commitment to protecting our world."

As I watched the ceremony, I felt a deep sense of reverence for the green core element and the Midori's connection to it. The display on the window slowly faded, and I turned to Lika, filled with newfound understanding and respect for the Midori.

Post seeing this, I felt overwhelm. I hold Lika's hand and said,

"Thank you for showing me this, Lika," I said, my voice filled with gratitude. "I feel like I understand the Midori much better now."

Lika smiled warmly. "I'm glad, Kenyzee. The Midori are a vital part of our world, and their abilities and wisdom are essential for maintaining the balance of Three Astral. Remember what you have learned today, and let it guide you on your journey."

## *The Journey Continues*

As we left the Viewing Window, I felt a renewed sense of purpose and determination. The path ahead was still uncertain, but with the knowledge and wisdom of the Midori and the support of Lika and Hijoka, I knew that there must be something based on their explanation. I feel like why they are giving so much of explanation about this. There must be something I should be responsible for.

We stepped outside into the vibrant world of Three Astral, the sights and sounds of the forest filling my senses. Lika led me through the village, pointing out various plants and creatures, explaining their roles in the ecosystem.

"The green core element connects us all," Lika said as we walked. "Every plant, every animal, every Greenion is linked by this energy. Our strength lies in our unity and our ability to work together to maintain the balance of our world."

As we walked, we encountered more members of the Midori community. They greeted Lika warmly and looked at me with curiosity and friendliness. It was clear that the Midori valued their sense of community and worked together to support one another.

One of the Greenions we met was a healer named Talara. She was tending to a group of injured animals, her hands glowing with green energy as she healed their wounds. Talara's touch was gentle and soothing, and the animals responded to her with trust and gratitude.

"Talara is one of our most skilled healers," Lika explained. "Her connection to the green core element allows her to heal injuries that would be fatal to others. She has a deep understanding of the energy that flows through all living things and uses it to bring about miraculous recoveries."

Talara smiled warmly at me. "Welcome, Kenyzee. It's an honor to meet you. If you ever need healing or guidance, please come to me. The green core element is a powerful force, and I am here to help you understand and harness it."

I thanked Talara, feeling a deep sense of appreciation for her kindness and wisdom. The more I learned about the Midori, the more I realized how interconnected their society was, each member playing a vital role in maintaining the balance and harmony of their world.

## *Embracing the Future*

As the day came to an end, Lika and I returned to the ancient structure. I felt a sense of fulfillment and anticipation for the journey ahead. The lessons I had learned about the Midori and their connection to the green core element had given me a new perspective on my own abilities and responsibilities.

Lika placed a hand on my shoulder, her expression filled with warmth and encouragement. "You have learned much today, Kenyzee. But remember, this is only the beginning. The journey ahead will be challenging, but with the support of the Midori and your connection to the green core element, you will find your place in this world."

Her words filled me with confidence and determination. I knew that my path was just beginning, and I was ready to embrace the challenges and opportunities that lay ahead. With the guidance of Lika, Hijoka, and the wisdom of the Midori, I felt prepared to face whatever the future held.

As I lay down to rest that night, I reflected on the day's events. The green core element's energy still pulsed within me, a reminder of the deep connection I now shared with the Midori. I closed my eyes, feeling a sense of peace and belonging, knowing that I was a part of something much larger than myself.

## Chapter - 6
# Journey to the Renions' Region (Kaji) and the Snonions' Region (Kori)

### *Morning with Lika*

The first light of dawn filtered into the room, casting a soft, warm glow over everything. I awoke feeling refreshed, the previous day's revelations still vivid in my mind. As I stretched and sat up, the door to my room opened, and Lika entered with a radiant smile.

"Good morning, Kenyzee," she greeted me. Her presence filled the room with warmth and light, and I couldn't help but notice how beautiful she looked in the morning light. Her hair shimmered like golden threads, and her eyes sparkled with kindness and wisdom.

"Good morning, Lika," I replied, feeling a wave of gratitude for her guidance and support. "You look... beautiful."

Lika blushed slightly and laughed softly. "Thank you, Kenyzee. Today, we have much to learn and explore. Are you ready for another journey?"

I nodded eagerly, my curiosity and excitement growing. "Yes, I am. What will we be learning about today?"

"Today, we will visit the Viewing Window again and learn about the Renions' Region (Kaji) and the Snonions' Region (Kori)," Lika explained. "These regions are home to the other two core elements – Red and Blue. Understanding their significance and the abilities of their inhabitants is crucial for your journey."

## *The Viewing Window*

Lika led me back to the room with the Viewing Window. The intricate designs and symbols around the window pulsed with energy, just as they had the day before. The window's surface shimmered and transformed into a vivid, three-dimensional display.

"This window will show us the past and present of the Renions' Region (Kaji) and the Snonions' Region (Kori)," Lika explained. "It will help you understand the unique characteristics and abilities of the inhabitants of these regions."

The window displayed a map of Three Astral, highlighting the two regions we were about to learn about. The Renions' Region (Kaji) was depicted in shades of red and orange, with volcanic landscapes and fiery rivers. The Snonions' Region (Kori) was shown in shades of blue and white, with icy landscapes and frozen lakes.

## *The Renions' Region (Kaji)*

Lika began to narrate the history and characteristics of the Renions' Region (Kaji). "The Renions' Region is deeply connected to the red core element, which represents fire and energy. This region is characterized by its volcanic landscapes, molten lava fields, and extreme temperatures."

As she spoke, the window displayed scenes of the Renions' Region. I saw towering volcanoes, rivers of flowing lava, and rugged mountains. The air seemed to shimmer with heat, and the ground was covered in ash and volcanic rock.

"The inhabitants of this region, known as the Renions, have developed unique abilities that allow them to thrive in this harsh environment," Lika continued. "They can manipulate fire and heat, using the energy of the red core element to their advantage. Their bodies are adapted to withstand extreme temperatures, and they possess incredible strength and resilience."

The window showed a Renion elder named Vulcanis, who was known for his mastery of the red core element. Vulcanis was a formidable figure, his body radiating with fiery energy. He moved with a powerful grace, his presence commanding respect and admiration.

"Vulcanis is one of the most respected elders in the Renions' Region," Lika explained. "He has lived for centuries, guiding the Renions with his knowledge and experience. His connection to the red core element is so strong that he can control the flow of lava and harness the energy of volcanoes."

I watched in awe as the window displayed Vulcanis leading a group of Renion warriors through the volcanic landscape. His presence seemed to calm the fiery environment, the lava and flames responding to his energy with a sense of order and control.

## *The Abilities of the Renions*

Lika continued to explain the unique abilities of the Renions. "The Renions can harness the energy of the red core element to perform incredible feats. Their powers include controlling fire, generating heat, and manipulating volcanic activity."

The window showed scenes of Renion warriors training in the volcanic landscape, their movements fluid and powerful. They were using their abilities to create barriers of fire, control the flow of lava, and withstand the intense heat of their environment.

"These warriors are trained to protect their region from threats," Lika said. "They are skilled in combat and can use their abilities to defend their land and people. The Renions are not only fierce warriors but also protectors of the natural balance of their environment."

One of the warriors, named Ignis, stood out in the display. He was a young and agile Renion, his body radiating with fiery energy. Ignis moved with incredible speed and precision, his connection to the red core element allowing him to anticipate and counter any attack.

"Ignis is one of our most promising young warriors," Lika said with a hint of pride. "He has a natural talent for using the red core element in combat. His agility and strength are unmatched, and he is deeply committed to protecting his region."

Ignis's movements were almost hypnotic, his agility making him seem more like a part of the volcanic landscape than a separate entity. He moved through the fiery terrain as if it were an extension of his own body, blending seamlessly into the environment. I watched in awe as he demonstrated his abilities, leaping from rock to rock with incredible grace and speed.

The window then shifted to show Ignis in a sparring match with another warrior. The intensity of their training was palpable, each move calculated and executed with precision. Ignis's ability to manipulate the environment to his advantage was remarkable. He used flames to entangle his opponent and created barriers of fire to protect himself.

### *The Role of the Renions in Society*

As the scenes continued to unfold, Lika explained the broader role of the Renions in their society. "The Renions are not only warriors but also leaders and innovators. They play a vital role in harnessing the energy of the red core element for various purposes, including energy production and technological advancements."

The window showed a Renion city, where the inhabitants were using the energy of the red core element to power their technology and infrastructure. The city was a marvel of engineering, with buildings made of volcanic rock and powered by geothermal energy.

"The Renions believe in using their abilities to improve their society and contribute to the overall prosperity of Three Astral," Lika said. "They teach the importance of innovation and progress, and their advancements in technology and energy production have had a significant impact on our world."

Another figure appeared in the display, a Renion elder named Pyra. She was a scientist and engineer, dedicated to developing new technologies that harnessed the energy of the red core element. Pyra spent her days in a laboratory, experimenting with different ways to use fire and heat for various applications.

"Pyra is one of our greatest innovators," Lika explained. "She has devoted her life to finding new ways to harness the energy of the red core element. Her work has led to numerous advancements in energy production, transportation, and technology."

Pyra was a dignified figure, her presence exuding a quiet strength and determination. She moved with deliberate care as she worked on her experiments, her dedication to innovation and progress evident in every meticulous action.

I watched as Pyra guided a group of young Renions through her laboratory. She showed them different experiments and technologies, each one a testament to her ingenuity and creativity. The young Renions were captivated by her teachings, their faces filled with curiosity and awe as they learned about the potential of the red core element.

### *The Snonions' Region (Kori)*

Lika then shifted her focus to the Snonions' Region (Kori). "The Snonions' Region is deeply connected to the blue core element, which represents ice and stability. This region is characterized by its icy landscapes, frozen lakes, and snow-covered plains."

As she spoke, the window displayed scenes of the Snonions' Region. I saw vast expanses of ice and snow, with majestic glaciers and frozen rivers. The air seemed to shimmer with cold, and the ground was covered in a thick layer of frost and ice.

"The inhabitants of this region, known as the Snonions, have developed unique abilities that allow them to thrive in this cold environment," Lika continued. "They can manipulate ice and cold, using the energy of the blue core element to their advantage. Their bodies are adapted to withstand extreme cold, and they possess incredible strength and resilience."

The window showed a Snonion elder named Glacius, who was known for his mastery of the blue core element. Glacius was a formidable figure, his body radiating with icy energy. He moved with a powerful grace, his presence commanding respect and admiration.

"Glacius is one of the most respected elders in the Snonions' Region," Lika explained. "He has lived for centuries, guiding the Snonions with his knowledge and experience. His connection to the blue core element is so strong that he can control the flow of ice and harness the energy of glaciers."

I watched in awe as the window displayed Glacius leading a group of Snonion warriors through the icy landscape. His presence seemed to calm the frigid environment, the ice and snow responding to his energy with a sense of order and control.

## *The Abilities of the Snonions*

Lika continued to explain the unique abilities of the Snonions. "The Snonions can harness the energy of the blue core element to perform incredible feats. Their powers include controlling ice, generating cold, and manipulating snow and frost."

The window showed scenes of Snonion warriors training in the icy landscape, their movements fluid and powerful. They were using their abilities to create barriers of ice, control the flow of snow, and withstand the intense cold of their environment.

"These warriors are trained to protect their region from threats," Lika said. "They are skilled in combat and can use their abilities to defend their land and people. The Snonions are not only fierce warriors but also protectors of the natural balance of their environment."

One of the warriors, named Frostine, stood out in the display. She was a youngest among all living being on this planet and agile Snonion, her body radiating with icy energy. Frostine moved with incredible precision, her connection to the blue core element allowing her to anticipate and counter any attack.

Frostine's movements were almost hypnotic, her agility making her seem more like a part of the icy landscape than a separate entity. She moved through the snowy terrain as if it were an extension of her own body, blending seamlessly into the environment. I watched in awe as she demonstrated her abilities, leaping from ice floe to ice floe with incredible grace and speed.

The window then shifted to show Frostine in a sparring match with another warrior. The intensity of their training was palpable, each move calculated and executed with precision. Frostine's ability to manipulate the environment to her advantage was remarkable. She used ice to entangle her opponent and created barriers of frost to protect herself.

## *The Role of the Snonions in Society*

As the scenes continued to unfold, Lika explained the broader role of the Snonions in their society. "The Snonions are not only warriors but also leaders and scholars. They play a vital role in maintaining the stability and order of their region, using their abilities to ensure that the natural balance is preserved."

The window showed a Snonion city, where the inhabitants were using the energy of the blue core element to create structures and infrastructure. The city was a marvel of engineering, with buildings made of ice and powered by the cold energy of the blue core element.

"The Snonions believe in using their abilities to improve their society and contribute to the overall stability of Three Astral," Lika said. "They teach the importance of order and discipline, and their advancements in architecture and environmental management have had a significant impact on our world."

Another figure appeared in the display, a Snonion elder named Glacia. She was a scholar and an environmentalist, dedicated to preserving the natural beauty and balance of the Snonions' Region. Glacia spent her days studying the glaciers and ice formations, ensuring that the region remained pristine and protected.

"Glacia is one of our greatest scholars," Lika explained. "She has devoted her life to understanding and preserving the natural environment of the Snonions' Region. Her work has led to numerous advancements in environmental protection and sustainability."

Glacia was a dignified figure, her presence exuding a quiet strength and determination. She moved with deliberate care as she studied the ice formations, her dedication to preserving the natural balance of the region evident in every meticulous action.

I watched as Glacia guided a group of young Snonions through the icy landscape. She showed them different ice formations and explained their significance, each one a testament to her knowledge and passion for the environment. The young Snonions were captivated by her teachings, their faces filled with curiosity and awe as they learned about the potential of the blue core element.

### *The Connection to the Blue Core*

Finally, Lika spoke about the deep connection between the Snonions and the blue core element. "The Snonions' abilities are directly linked to the blue core. Their connection allows them to draw upon its energy and use it to control and manipulate ice and cold."

The window displayed a sacred ceremony, where Snonion elders and warriors gathered around the blue core element. They placed their hands on the orb, their bodies glowing with blue light as they absorbed its energy. The scene was both awe-inspiring and humbling, a testament to the power of the blue core and the unity of the Snonions.

"This ceremony is a vital part of our culture," Lika explained. "It reinforces the bond between the Snonions and the blue core element. By connecting with the core, they renew their strength and commitment to protecting our world."

As I watched the ceremony, I felt a deep sense of reverence for the blue core element and the Snonions' connection to it. The display on the window slowly faded, and I turned to Lika, filled with newfound understanding and respect for the Snonions.

"Thank you for showing me this, Lika," I said, my voice filled with gratitude. "I feel like I understand the Snonions much better now."

Lika smiled warmly. "I'm glad, Kenyzee. The Snonions are a vital part of our world, and their abilities and wisdom are essential for maintaining the balance of Three Astral. Remember what you have learned today, and let it guide you on your journey."

### *The Journey Continues*

As we left the Viewing Window, I felt a renewed sense of purpose and determination. The path ahead was still uncertain, but with the knowledge and wisdom of the Renions and Snonions and the support of Lika and Hijoka, I will be safe here.

"The core elements connect us all," Lika said as we walked. "Every plant, every animal, every Greenion,

Renion, and Snonion is linked by this energy. Our strength lies in our unity and our ability to work together to maintain the balance of our world."

As we walked, we encountered more members of the Renion and Snonion communities. They greeted Lika warmly and looked at me with curiosity and friendliness. It was clear that these communities valued their sense of unity and worked together to support one another.

One of the Renions we met was a healer named Ember. She was tending to a group of injured Renions, her hands glowing with fiery energy as she healed their wounds. Ember's touch was gentle and soothing, and the injured Renions responded to her with trust and gratitude.

### *Embracing the Future*

As the day came to an end, Lika and I returned to the ancient structure. I felt a sense of fulfillment and anticipation for the journey ahead. The lessons I had learned about the Renions and Snonions and their connections to the red and blue core elements had given me a new perspective on my own abilities and responsibilities.

Lika placed a hand on my shoulder, her expression filled with warmth and encouragement. "You have learned much today, Kenyzee. But remember, this is only the beginning. The journey ahead will be challenging, but with the support of the Renions, Snonions, and your connection to the core elements, you will find your place in this world."

Her words filled me with confidence and determination. I knew that my path was just beginning, and I was ready to embrace the challenges and opportunities that lay ahead. With the guidance of Lika, Hijoka, and the wisdom of the Renions and Snonions, I felt prepared to face whatever the future held.

As I lay down to rest that night, I reflected on the day's events. The energy of the core elements still pulsed within me, a reminder of the deep connections I now shared with the inhabitants of Three Astral. I closed my eyes, feeling a sense of peace and belonging, knowing that I was a part of something much larger than myself.

The journey to the Renions' Region (Kaji) and the Snonions' Region (**Midori**) had not only revealed the power and wisdom of the Renions and Snonions but had also shown me the importance of unity, balance, and harmony. With this newfound understanding, I was ready to continue my journey on Three Astral, confident that I could make a difference and fulfill my destiny.

---

## *Turn To Chapter 8: Left Hand Side (Page no. 55)*

---

## Chapter - 7
# Resume Dream

### *Awakening in a Dream*

The effects of the Jikoya drug were both overwhelming and enlightening. As I lay on my bed, my body numb and my mind adrift, I felt a strange sensation wash over me. It was as if the barrier between my conscious mind and my dreams had dissolved, allowing me to step into a realm that was both familiar and alien. The vivid colors and ethereal beauty of Three Astral surrounded me once more, but this time, there was a sense of clarity and purpose that had been missing before.

I found myself reliving the moments of my seizure, the 166 seconds that had seemed to stretch into eternity. The memories were fragmented and disjointed, but as I focused, they began to coalesce into a coherent narrative. I could see the vibrant landscapes of Three Astral, feel the pulsating energy of the core elements, and hear the faint whispers of the plants and stones.

The world around me seemed to pulse with life, each element resonating with a unique energy that I could feel deep within my being. The connection was undeniable, a thread that linked me to this otherworldly realm in a way that defied explanation. As I navigated through the dreamscape, I realized that this was more than just a hallucination – it was a glimpse into a reality that existed parallel to my own.

I wandered through the dream, taking in the sights and sounds of Three Astral. The colors were more vivid than anything I had ever seen, the air filled with a palpable sense of magic. Every step I took felt significant, as if I were treading on sacred ground. The plants and creatures around me seemed to recognize my presence, their movements filled with a strange familiarity. It was as if they were welcoming me back, acknowledging my return to a place that felt like home.

The memories of my seizure began to blend with my current experience, creating a seamless transition between past and present. I could see the faces of the beings I had encountered, their expressions etched with a mix of curiosity and recognition. Their eyes seemed to hold a depth of knowledge that went beyond words, a silent understanding of the journey I was on.

### *Understanding Midori, Kaji, and Kori*

As I continued to explore the dreamscape, the lessons I had learned from Lika about the three core elements came flooding back. I remembered the journey to the Green Core, the awe-inspiring power it held, and the connection I felt with the plants and creatures of Midori. The lush, verdant landscapes of the Green Core were a testament to the life-giving energy that flowed through every living being in the region.

The Green Core was not just a source of power; it was the heartbeat of Midori. The plants seemed to thrive in its presence, their leaves and branches reaching out to absorb the energy that emanated from the core. The creatures of Midori, too, were intricately connected to the Green Core. Their movements were graceful and fluid, reflecting the harmony that existed between them and the natural world.

I recalled the fiery landscapes of Riko, the molten lava and the relentless heat, and the resilience of the beings who thrived there. The Red Core was a force of raw, untamed power, shaping the environment with its intense energy. The creatures of Kaji were adapted to the harsh conditions, their bodies built to withstand the extreme temperatures and constant upheaval.

The Kaji were a formidable people, their strength and determination forged in the crucible of their fiery homeland. They possessed a deep connection to the Red Core, drawing on its power to fuel their own abilities. The lava flows and volcanic eruptions were a constant reminder of the dynamic nature of their world, a place where change was the only constant.

And I remembered the icy expanses of Kori, the stark beauty of the frozen world, and the strength of the creatures that called it home. The Blue Core was a source of stability and tranquility, its cool energy providing a sense of calm amidst the harsh conditions. The beings of Kori were hardy and resilient, their lives shaped by the frozen landscapes that surrounded them.

The Kori were a people of wisdom and patience, their strength lying in their ability to endure and adapt. The ice and snow that blanketed their world were both a challenge and a source of beauty, a reflection of the delicate balance that existed in their lives. The Blue Core was a beacon of hope, its steady energy a reminder of the enduring spirit of the Kori.

Each core element was unique, but together they formed a delicate balance that sustained the planet of Three Astral. The interconnectedness of the elements was a testament to the harmony that could be achieved through diversity and cooperation. It was a lesson that resonated deeply with me, a reminder of the potential for unity in the face of adversity.

The more I learned about the core elements, the more I understood their significance. They were not just sources of power; they were the lifeblood of Three Astral, the foundation upon which the entire world was built. The balance between the core elements was crucial to maintaining the stability of the planet, and any disruption to this balance could have catastrophic consequences.

### *Seeking Purpose*

With this newfound understanding, I felt a growing sense of urgency to uncover the truth about myself and my purpose. I needed answers, and I knew that Lika was the key to unlocking them. As if sensing my thoughts, she appeared before me, her presence a comforting beacon in the surreal landscape of my dreams.

"Lika," I called out, my voice trembling with a mixture of anticipation and fear. "I need to know more about myself. Why am I here? What is my purpose?"

Lika's eyes softened with understanding, and she took my hand in hers. "Kenyzee, you are here because you have a unique connection to the core elements. Your presence on

Three Astral is not a coincidence. There is a reason why you have been drawn to this world, and it is tied to the dark matter that threatens our planet."

Her words resonated deeply within me, and I felt a sense of clarity beginning to form. The hallucinations, the seizures, the visions – they were all pieces of a puzzle that was slowly coming together. I realized that my connection to Three Astral was not just a random occurrence, but a crucial part of a larger plan.

Lika continued, her voice filled with a mixture of sadness and determination. "Dark matter is a force of chaos and destruction. It destabilizes the balance of the core elements, causing disruptions that threaten the very fabric of our world. It has already claimed many lives, including those of my parents."

## *The Dark Matter Threat*

Lika's expression grew somber as she began to explain the situation. "Dark matter is a force of chaos and destruction. It destabilizes the balance of the core elements, causing disruptions that threaten the very fabric of our world. It has already claimed many lives, including those of my parents."

Her voice cracked with emotion, and I could see the pain etched on her face. The memory of her parent's deaths was a wound that had not healed, a source of grief that she carried with her every day. I felt a surge of empathy for her, a deep connection that transcended the boundaries of our respective worlds.

"My parents were brave and selfless," Lika continued, her voice trembling. "They dedicated their lives to protecting Three Astral from the dark matter. They understood the importance of maintaining the balance of the core elements, and they sacrificed everything to preserve it. But in the end, it wasn't enough. The dark matter took them from me, and it continues to spread, threatening everything we hold dear."

Lika's eyes glistened with tears, and I could feel the depth of her sorrow. The loss of her parents had left a void in her life, a pain that was palpable even in the dreamscape. It was a reminder that the struggle against the dark matter was not just a fight for survival, but a battle for the very soul of Three Astral.

"The dark matter is relentless," Lika said, her voice steadying. "It corrodes everything it touches, disrupting the harmony of our world. The balance of the core elements is delicate, and even a small disturbance can have catastrophic effects. The dark matter has already caused rifts and fractures, and if it continues unchecked, it could lead to the complete destabilization of our planet."

### *The Emotional Toll*

Lika's words struck a chord within me, resonating with my own sense of loss and longing. I could feel the weight of her sorrow, the burden of her grief. It was a reminder that the struggles we faced were not just abstract concepts, but deeply personal battles that shaped our lives in profound ways.

"Lika, I'm so sorry," I said softly, squeezing her hand. "I can't imagine the pain you've been through. But I want to help. I want to be a part of the solution."

Tears welled up in Lika's eyes, and she nodded gratefully. "Thank you, Kenyzee. Your willingness to help means more to me than you can imagine. Together, we can find a way to stop the dark matter and restore balance to our world."

As we stood there, hand in hand, I felt a renewed sense of purpose. The journey ahead would be difficult, but I was no longer alone. With Lika by my side, I was ready to face whatever challenges lay ahead. The dream memory had shown me the path, and now it was up to me to follow it.

Lika's determination was contagious, and I felt a surge of resolve. The connection between us was undeniable, a bond forged through shared experiences and mutual understanding. We were both fighting for something greater than ourselves, a cause that transcended the boundaries of our respective worlds.

The emotional toll of the struggle was immense, but it was also a source of strength. The memories of those we had lost, the sacrifices that had been made, fueled our determination to succeed. The fight against the dark matter was not just a battle for survival, but a quest for justice and balance.

As I looked into Lika's eyes, I saw the fire of her resolve. She was a beacon of hope, a reminder that even in the darkest of times, there was light to be found. Her strength and courage inspired me, giving me the resolve to continue the journey ahead.

We stood there for what felt like an eternity, our hands clasped together, drawing strength from each other's presence. The world of Three Astral seemed to fade into the background, leaving only the bond between us, a connection that transcended the boundaries of reality and dream.

Lika's voice broke the silence, filled with a sense of quiet determination. "Kenyzee, there is much we need to do. The journey ahead will be fraught with challenges, but I believe in you. Together, we can find a way to restore balance to our world and put an end to the threat of the dark matter."

Her words resonated deeply within me, filling me with a sense of purpose and determination. The path ahead was uncertain, but I knew that I was not alone. With Lika by my side, I felt ready to face whatever challenges lay ahead.

## Chapter - 8
# Formation of G-Four Astral

### *The Most Beautiful Place*

The morning on Three Astral was unlike any I had ever experienced on Earth. The air was vibrant and infused with the unique energy of the core elements, filled with the otherworldly scents of exotic flora and the distinct vibrations of Three Astral's life force. There was a vitality to it, an energy that seemed to seep into my very being. As I stood with Lika, preparing to embark on our journey to what she described as the most beautiful place on the planet, I felt a sense of anticipation and excitement building within me.

The path we took was lined with vibrant flora, their colors more vivid than anything I had ever seen. The core elements – Green, Red, and Blue – provided the light and energy that sustained the planet, casting a radiant glow over everything. The sky above us was a deep, serene greenish, with wisps of clouds that seemed to dance in harmony with the gentle breeze. The atmosphere was charged with a subtle hum, a background symphony that resonated with the core elements.

Lika walked beside me, her presence a comforting constant. Her serene demeanor and the subtle glow that seemed to emanate from her made me feel safe and at ease. She moved with a grace and confidence that was both reassuring and inspiring. I couldn't help but marvel at the world around me, the intricate details of the plants, the harmonious symphony of nature's sounds, and the vibrant energy that permeated the air. Every step brought us closer to our destination, and with each step, I felt a growing connection to the land and its energies.

Finally, we reached a clearing that opened up to a breathtaking vista. The landscape before us was a tapestry of rolling hills, crystalline lakes, and towering trees that seemed to touch the sky. The core elements' energy radiated in gentle waves, their distinct auras adding to the mesmerizing beauty of the scene. The Green Core's energy created a lush, verdant landscape, the Red Core's energy added a dynamic intensity, and the Blue Core's energy provided a calming stability.

Lika gestured for me to sit on a large, smooth rock that overlooked the panorama. As I settled into place, I closed my eyes and took a deep breath, allowing the tranquility of the environment to wash over me. It was then that I felt it – a subtle vibration that resonated deep within me. It was as if the very essence of the core elements was flowing through me, filling me with a sense of unity and harmony.

"I can feel it," I whispered, opening my eyes to meet Lika's gaze. "I can feel the vibration of all the core elements."

Lika's face lit up with a radiant smile, her eyes shimmering with joy. "I'm so happy to hear that, Kenyzee.

It means that you are truly connected to the essence of Three Astral."

The sensation was unlike anything I had ever felt before. It was as if my entire being was attuned to the energies of the core elements. The Green Core's energy was life-giving and nurturing, the Red Core's energy was raw and untamed, and the Blue Core's energy was calm and stabilizing. Together, they created a harmonious symphony that resonated within me, a reminder of the interconnectedness of all life on Three Astral.

Lika sat beside me, her expression thoughtful. "This place is special," she said softly. "It's a place where the energies of the core elements converge, creating a unique harmony. It's no wonder you can feel their vibrations so strongly here."

I nodded, absorbing her words. The beauty of the landscape and the intensity of the core elements' energy were overwhelming. It was a place of profound significance, a testament to the power and balance that sustained life on Three Astral.

As we sat together, taking in the beauty of the surroundings, Lika began to explain the importance of the core elements and the balance they created. "The core elements are the lifeblood of our planet," she said. "They provide the energy and stability that sustain all life on Three Astral. Each element – Green, Red, and Blue – has its own unique properties and contributions, but it is their balance that is crucial."

Her words were both enlightening and humbling. I realized that the core elements were more than just sources of power; they were the foundation upon which the entire planet was built. The balance between them was delicate, and any disruption could have catastrophic consequences.

Lika's expression grew more serious as she continued. "The balance between the core elements is not just a matter of survival," she explained. "It is the foundation of our entire world. The harmony between the Green, Red, and Blue Cores ensures that life can thrive in its diverse forms. If this balance is disrupted, the consequences could be catastrophic."

I listened intently, feeling a growing sense of responsibility. "But how can we maintain this balance?" I asked, my voice tinged with urgency.

Lika's gaze softened as she placed a reassuring hand on my shoulder. "That's where you come in, Kenyzee. You were created with a unique purpose – to sense and feel the core elements in a way that no one else can. You have the ability to detect even the slightest disturbances and to help restore balance when it is threatened."

Her words filled me with a mix of awe and trepidation. "How was I created?" I asked, my curiosity piqued.

Lika took a deep breath, her expression thoughtful. "You were not born naturally like the rest of us. Brilliant minds from all regions came together to create you, using advanced biotechnology and a combination of DNA from the Greenions, Renions, and Snonions. The goal was to create a being who could bridge the gap between the core elements and maintain the delicate balance that sustains our world."

Her words were both humbling and daunting. "So, I was created for this purpose?" I asked, trying to wrap my mind around the enormity of it all.

"Yes," Lika replied softly. "You were designed to be sensitive to the core elements, to feel their vibrations and to understand their needs. This ability makes you uniquely suited to help us in our fight against the dark matter. It's a great responsibility, but it also means that you are an integral part of our world."

As I processed her words, a sense of determination began to build within me. "But why me? Why was I chosen for this role?"

Lika's eyes met mine, her gaze unwavering. "You have a unique connection to the core elements, Kenyzee. Your presence here is not a coincidence – it is a testament to the brilliance and dedication of those who created you. They saw in you the potential to be a force for good, to help us protect our world from the threat of dark matter."

As Lika spoke, I felt a renewed sense of purpose. The vibrations of the core elements continued to pulse through me, each one distinct yet interconnected. It was as if I could feel the heartbeat of the planet itself, a rhythm that resonated deep within my soul.

"You have the ability to sense the core elements," Lika continued. "This means that you can detect even the slightest changes in their energy. It's a gift that allows you to understand the balance of our world in a way that no one else can."

I closed my eyes, focusing on the vibrations that flowed through me. Each element had its own unique frequency, a signature that was both familiar and foreign.

Lika's voice was a soothing presence as she continued to explain. "The core elements are more than just sources of power – they are the essence of our world. By understanding their vibrations, you can help us maintain the balance that is so crucial to our survival."

Her words resonated deeply within me, and I felt a sense of clarity and purpose. "I want to help," I said, my voice filled with determination. "I want to do whatever it takes to protect our world from the dark matter."

Lika's eyes softened with gratitude as she squeezed my hand. "Thank you, Kenyzee. Your willingness to help means more than you can imagine. Together, we can find a way to restore balance and protect our world."

The bond between us grew stronger with each passing moment. Lika's presence was a source of comfort and strength, and I felt a deep connection to her and to the world of Three Astral. The journey ahead would be challenging, but I knew that I was not alone.

As I sat there, surrounded by the beauty of the landscape and the vibrations of the core elements, I felt a profound sense of purpose. The memories of my seizure and the visions of Three Astral had led me to this moment, and I was ready to embrace my role in the fight against the dark matter.

The path ahead was uncertain, but with Lika by my side, I felt ready to face whatever challenges lay ahead. The balance of the core elements was crucial to the survival of our world, and I was determined to do everything in my power to protect it.

As the core elements continued to radiate their energy, I felt a deep connection to the world around me. The journey to this beautiful place had opened my eyes to the intricate balance that sustained life on Three Astral. It was a reminder of the interconnectedness of all things and the importance of maintaining harmony in the face of adversity.

With Lika's guidance and the support of those who believed in me, I felt ready to take on the responsibility of protecting our world. The journey ahead would be filled with challenges, but I was determined to fulfill my purpose and restore balance to the core elements.

### *The Importance of Balance*

Lika's expression grew more serious as she began to explain the significance of the balance between the core elements. "The balance between the core elements is crucial for the stability of our planet," she said. "Each element contributes to the harmony that sustains life on Three Astral. If this balance is disrupted, it creates a void that dark matter can exploit."

I listened intently, absorbing her words. The core elements were more than just sources of power; they were the foundation upon which the entire planet was built. The balance between them was delicate, and any disruption could have catastrophic consequences.

"The core elements are like the threads of a tapestry," Lika continued. "Each thread is vital, and if one is removed or weakened, the entire tapestry begins to unravel. Dark matter is a force of chaos and destruction, and it seeks out these weaknesses to gain a foothold."

Her voice trembled slightly as she spoke of the dark matter. "It corrodes and destabilizes the core elements, spreading its influence like a disease. If left unchecked, it will consume everything in its path, leaving nothing but ruin in its wake. This is why maintaining the balance is so important – it is the only way to protect our world from being overwhelmed by dark matter."

The weight of her words settled heavily on me, and I felt a newfound sense of responsibility. "But how can we maintain this balance?" I asked, my voice tinged with urgency.

Lika's expression grew more thoughtful as she continued to explain the intricacies of the core elements and their balance. "The Green Core provides the life-giving energy that sustains all plant life on Three Astral. It is the source of growth and vitality, nurturing the flora and fauna that make up our ecosystems."

I closed my eyes, focusing on the Green Core's energy. I could feel its nurturing presence, a warm and vibrant force that pulsed through the landscape. It was a reminder of the interconnectedness of all living things, a testament to the power of nature and its ability to sustain life.

"The Red Core, on the other hand," Lika said, her voice taking on a more intense tone, "is the source of raw, untamed power. It fuels the dynamic processes that shape our world, from volcanic eruptions to the movement of tectonic plates. It is the energy of creation and destruction, a force that must be harnessed with care."

The Red Core's energy was intense and powerful, a fiery force that radiated through the ground beneath me. It was a reminder of the dynamic processes that shaped the planet, the constant cycle of creation and destruction that was essential to the evolution of life.

"And then there is the Blue Core," Lika continued, her voice calming. "The Blue Core provides stability and tranquility. Its energy is cool and steady, bringing balance to the chaotic forces of the Red Core. It is the foundation upon which our world is built, a source of calm amidst the storm."

The Blue Core's energy was soothing and stabilizing, a calming presence that balanced the intense forces of the other core elements. It was a reminder of the importance of stability and harmony, a beacon of hope in the face of chaos.

As Lika spoke, I felt a deep connection to the core elements and the balance they created. The harmony between them was crucial to the survival of our world, and I was determined to do everything in my power to protect it.

"But how do we maintain this balance?" I asked, my voice filled with determination.

Lika's gaze softened as she placed a reassuring hand on my shoulder. "It is not an easy task, Kenyzee. It requires constant vigilance and a deep understanding of the core elements and their interactions. That is why you were created – to help us detect disturbances and restore balance when it is threatened."

Her words filled me with a sense of purpose and resolve. The journey ahead would be challenging, but I was ready to embrace my role in the fight against the dark matter. The balance of the core elements was crucial to the survival of our world, and I was determined to do everything in my power to protect it.

As we sat together, taking in the beauty of the landscape and the vibrations of the core elements, I felt a profound sense of purpose. The memories of my seizure and the visions of Three Astral had led me to this moment, and I was ready to embrace my role in the fight against the dark matter.

The core elements continued to radiate their energy, filling the air with a subtle hum that resonated deep within me. The journey to this beautiful place had opened my eyes to the intricate balance that sustained life on Three Astral. It was a reminder of the interconnectedness of all things and the importance of maintaining harmony in the face of adversity.

### *The Creation of Kenyzee*

As the realization of my role in maintaining the balance of the core elements sank in, a multitude of questions began to form in my mind. The most pressing of these was the nature of my creation. How had I come to exist in this world, and what had led to my unique abilities?

Lika seemed to sense my curiosity. She took a deep breath, her expression thoughtful. "The story of your creation is a remarkable one, Kenyzee. It is a testament to the brilliance and dedication of the scientists and researchers from all regions of Three Astral. They came together with a singular purpose: to create a being capable of bridging the gap between the core elements and maintaining the delicate balance that sustains our world."

Her words filled me with a mix of awe and trepidation. "So, how was I created?" I asked, my curiosity piqued.

As I processed her words, a sense of determination began to build within me. "But why me? Why was I chosen for this role?"

Lika continued her explanation, her voice filled with reverence for the scientists who had created me. "The process of your creation was complex and required the collaboration of brilliant minds from all regions. They combined their knowledge of biotechnology, genetics, and the core elements to create a being who could bridge the gap between the elements."

I marveled at the ingenuity and dedication of these scientists. "So, they used DNA from the Greenions, Renions, and Snonions to create me?"

"Yes," Lika confirmed. "Each region contributed its unique qualities to your creation.

"The Greenions provided their nurturing and life-giving qualities, the Renions contributed their raw power and dynamism, and the Snonions added their stability and calming presence. By combining these distinct attributes, the scientists were able to create a being who embodied the strengths of all three regions."

As I absorbed this information, a question formed in my mind. "But if I was created using such advanced technology and combined DNA, why did it take so long for me to come to life?"

Lika's expression grew more serious. "That is the most extraordinary part of your story, Kenyzee. While the scientists were able to create your physical form, they could not imbue you with the essence of life – a soul. They realized that your existence required more than just biological components; it needed a spark, a perfect frequency that would resonate with your being and bring you to life."

I listened intently, fascinated by the concept. "A perfect frequency?"

"Yes," Lika continued. "The scientists theorized that a perfect frequency, one that harmonized with the vibrations of the core elements, would ignite the spark of life within you. They believed that when this frequency resonated with your body, you would come alive."

The notion was both intriguing and mystifying. "So, I was essentially waiting for this perfect frequency to be found?"

Lika nodded. "Exactly. For ten long years, your body lay dormant, a testament to the hope and faith of the scientists who created you. They never gave up, believing that one day, the perfect frequency would resonate with your being and awaken you."

Her words sent a shiver down my spine. "And it took ten years for that to happen?"

"Yes," Lika confirmed. "For a decade, your body remained in stasis, waiting for the moment when the perfect frequency would bring you to life. And then, one day, it happened. The core elements aligned, the perfect frequency was achieved, and you awoke."

The realization was overwhelming. I had been created for a specific purpose, designed to maintain the balance of the core elements and protect Three Astral from the dark matter. After ten years of dormancy, the perfect frequency had finally brought me to life.

As I sat there, processing the enormity of what Lika had told me, a sense of determination and resolve began to take hold. The responsibility of my existence was immense, but I felt a deep connection to this world and a desire to fulfill my role.

Lika's voice was gentle as she continued. "Your creation is a testament to the brilliance and dedication of those who believed in you. They saw the potential for greatness within you, and they trusted that one day, you would awaken and fulfill your purpose."

Her words filled me with a sense of purpose and resolve. The journey ahead would be challenging, but I was ready to embrace my role in the fight against the dark matter. The balance of the core elements was crucial to the survival of our world, and I was determined to do everything in my power to protect it.

I nodded, feeling the weight of her words. The core elements were the lifeblood of Three Astral, and their balance was essential to the stability of the planet. The threat of dark matter was a reminder of the fragility of this balance, a force that sought to destabilize and destroy the harmony that sustained life.

"But how do we maintain this balance?" I asked, my voice filled with determination.

## Chapter - 9
# Confused

### *The Weight of Reality*

The gentle glow of the core elements continued to illuminate the landscape of Three Astral as I sat with Lika, the weight of our conversation settling heavily on my shoulders. Understanding why I was connected to Kenyzee and the importance of my role in maintaining the balance of the core elements filled me with a sense of responsibility, but also with an overwhelming sense of confusion and fear.

"I don't want to stay here," I blurted out, my voice shaking. "I need help, Lika. I need to go back to my real life."

Lika looked at me with concern, her eyes softening. "Kenyzee, I understand this is a lot to take in. But you are crucial to our fight against the dark matter. Your unique abilities are our best hope."

Her words, though meant to reassure, only heightened my anxiety. "I understand why I'm connected to Kenyzee," I said, my voice trembling. "It's because G-Four Astral and Kenyzee's body's frequency matches my soul's frequency when I have seizures. But this... all of this, it feels like I'm just seeing dreams that have already happened. I'm confused about what's real."

Lika reached out and placed a comforting hand on my shoulder. "I know it's overwhelming, but you have to trust that you are here for a reason."

I shook my head, tears welling up in my eyes. "What if I can't stop the dark matter? What if I fail and this whole planet gets destroyed because of me? And what about my family back on Earth? If I die here, Lika, you said my real body would become like I'm in a coma. I can't do that to them."

Lika's expression grew more serious. "Yes, if you die here, your body on Earth would enter a coma-like state. But you have a unique opportunity to make a difference here, Kenyzee. Your family would want you to do what's right."

I thought about my parents, my sister, and all the moments we had shared. The thought of them losing me, or me being stuck in a coma, was unbearable. "I can't," I whispered. "I can't stay here. I need to go back to my place where my real life is."

Lika's face showed a mix of understanding and sadness. "If that is truly what you want, we will find a way. But please consider the impact you could have here. You have a chance to save so many lives."

The conflict within me was tearing me apart. I wanted to help Lika and the people of Three Astral, but my fear for my family's well-being and my own confusion about reality were too overwhelming. "I'm sorry, Lika," I said, my voice breaking. "I just want to go home."

The weight of my words hung in the air, creating a palpable tension between us. I could see the disappointment in Lika's eyes, but also a deep understanding. She knew that my heart was torn between two worlds and that my decision was not made lightly

## *Torn Between Two Worlds*

The days that followed were filled with an unbearable stress. I spent hours pacing the beautiful landscapes of Three Astral, my mind a whirlwind of thoughts and emotions. The beauty of this world contrasted sharply with the turmoil within me.

Lika stayed close, offering support and guidance, but my mind kept drifting back to Earth. The more I thought about my family, the more desperate I became to return to my real life. The connection to Kenyzee, though fascinating, felt like a burden I wasn't ready to bear.

"I don't belong here," I confided to Lika one evening as we sat by a tranquil lake, its waters reflecting the soft glow of the core elements. "I belong with my family. They need me, and I need them."

Lika nodded slowly, her eyes filled with empathy. "I understand, Kenyzee. It's natural to feel that way. But you have to understand, your presence here is not just a coincidence. There is a purpose to it."

Her words, though sincere, did little to quell the storm of emotions inside me. "I can't just abandon them," I said, my voice rising with frustration. "I can't leave my family behind. They need to know I'm okay."

Lika placed a reassuring hand on mine. "We will find a way, Kenyzee. But you need to trust that you are here for a reason. You have the power to make a difference."

The weight of her words pressed down on me, but my mind was made up. "I need to go back," I repeated, more firmly this time. "Please, Lika, help me get back to my real life."

The tension between my desire to help and my longing to return to my family created a rift within me. I felt like I was being pulled in two directions, each with its own set of responsibilities and emotions. The connection to Kenyzee and the core elements was undeniable, but my love for my family was equally powerful.

### *Confronting the Reality*

Despite Lika's efforts to help me understand my role and the importance of my presence on Three Astral, my determination to return to Earth only grew stronger. The more I thought about my family, the more desperate I became to see them again.

One morning, as the soft glow of the core elements filled the air, I approached Lika with a sense of urgency. "Lika, I need to go back. Please, I can't stay here any longer."

Lika looked at me, her expression a mix of concern and resolve. "Kenyzee, you have to understand the consequences. If you leave now, we may lose our best chance to stop the dark matter."

Her words struck a chord of fear within me, but the thought of my family being left without me was too much to bear. "I understand the risks," I said, my voice trembling. "But I can't do this. I can't stay here and fight a battle that might not even be real. My family needs me."

Lika sighed, her eyes reflecting the weight of the decision. "If that is truly what you want, we will find a way to send you back. But please, Kenyzee, think about the lives you could save here."

The conflict within me was almost unbearable. I wanted to help, but my fear and confusion were too overwhelming. "I have to go back," I said firmly. "I need to be with my family."

Lika's expression softened as she placed a comforting hand on my shoulder. "I understand, Kenyzee. Your feelings are valid, and your desire to be with your family is completely natural. We will find a way to send you back."

Her words provided a sense of relief, but also a deep sadness. The thought of leaving behind the people I had come to care about on Three Astral weighed heavily on my heart. But my resolve to return to Earth was unwavering.

### *The Final Moments*

The day of my departure arrived all too quickly. As I stood with Lika in the clearing where my journey had begun, the reality of what I was leaving behind hit me with full force.

"Are you sure about this, Kenyzee?" Lika asked, her eyes searching mine for any hint of doubt.

I nodded, though my heart ached with the weight of the decision. "I'm sure. I need to be with my family. But I'll never forget what I've learned here."

Lika smiled, though her eyes were filled with sadness. "Thank you, Kenyzee. For everything. Your presence here has made a difference, even if you don't realize it yet."

As the process to send me back to Earth began, I felt a mixture of relief and sorrow. The connection to Three Astral, to Lika, and to the core elements would always be a part of me, but my place was with my family.

With a final wave, I felt the familiar pull of the transition, and the world around me began to blur. My last thoughts were of gratitude and hope – gratitude for the experiences I had gained, and hope that I could find a way to help both worlds in the future.

As I began to fade, Lika's voice reached out to me one last time. "Kenyzee, just before you go, I need to share something important with you..."

# Chapter – 10
# Lika Lost Everything

### *The Decision to Leave*

After our intense conversation, Lika sighed deeply, her shoulders slumping as if a great weight had been placed upon them. "Kenyzee, I understand your decision," she said softly. "If returning to Earth is what you truly desire, I will help you. You deserve to be happy."

I nodded, feeling a mixture of relief and sorrow. ," I said, my voice trembling. "But before I go, I want to understand more about you and why you're so committed to this cause."

Lika gave a faint smile, her eyes reflecting a deep well of sadness. "Very well, Kenyzee. Let me tell you my story."

She paused for a moment, gathering her thoughts. The air around us was filled with the soft hum of the core elements, their glow casting a gentle light on Lika's face. It was a face marked by strength and resilience, but also by a profound sadness that seemed to go beyond words.

Lika's face softened as she began to speak, her voice trembling slightly with the weight of her memories. "I lived on the edge of the green core region," she began, her eyes distant as if she were looking back through the mists of time. "It was a small village that thrived on the life-giving energy of the green core. My family was happy. I had a sister and a brother named Nazy, who dreamed of becoming a warrior. Our parents were kind and loving, and our village was a place of peace and joy."

Her voice grew softer as she continued. "Nazy was always the adventurous one, always eager to protect and serve. He was strong and brave, and we all believed he would achieve great things. Our days were filled with laughter and love, and I cherished every moment we spent together."

Lika's eyes glistened with tears as she spoke of her family. "My sister was my best friend. We would spend hours exploring the forests and fields around our village, discovering new plants and animals. Our parents were the heart of our family, always there with a kind word or a helping hand. They taught us the importance of community and caring for one another."

A shadow crossed her face as she recalled the darker times. "But one day, everything changed. The stability of our planet suddenly shifted. The energy we received from the core elements began to change, corrupted by the presence of dark matter. It was as if the very essence of our world was being twisted and distorted."

Her voice wavered as she described the onset of chaos. "As the energy from the core elements changed, so did the behavior of the creatures living on the edge of the green core region. They began to act like zombies, their minds clouded by the dark influence. Our once peaceful village was thrown into chaos, and the people I loved started to behave like mindless creatures, driven by a primal, destructive force."

## *Life on the Edge of the Green Core*

Lika's voice trembled as she continued. "At first, we didn't understand what was happening. People we had known all our lives began to turn on each other, their eyes filled with a terrifying emptiness. It was as if they were no longer themselves, but rather vessels for some malevolent force."

Her tears flowed freely now, and I felt a deep sense of empathy for her. "But you were unaffected," I said, trying to understand.

Lika nodded. "Yes, I was the only one who remained unaffected. At first, I couldn't understand why. It seemed like a cruel twist of fate that spared me while everyone around me fell victim to the dark influence."

She paused, taking a deep breath before continuing. "The days that followed were a nightmare. Our village was torn apart by violence and fear. My brother Nazy, who had always been so full of life and dreams, became one of the zombies. In his mindless state, he attacked our village, killing everyone, including our parents and my sister. It was a nightmare that I couldn't escape from. My mom and dad used green telepathy to transfer me to a safer place within the green core, sacrificing themselves to ensure my survival."

Lika's tears flowed freely now, her pain and sorrow palpable. "I survived, but at what cost? I lost everything that mattered to me. My family, my village, my sense of safety—all gone in an instant. The guilt and grief were overwhelming, but I knew I had to keep going. I had to find a way to prevent this from happening to anyone else."

I felt a deep sense of empathy for Lika, understanding now why she was so dedicated to stopping the dark matter. "I'm so sorry, Lika," I said softly. "I can't imagine the pain you've been through."

Lika wiped her tears, her expression determined. "That's why I fight, Kenyzee. To make sure no one else has to endure what I did. To restore balance to our world and protect those who cannot protect themselves."

Her story left me deeply moved, and I struggled with my own conflicting emotions. On one hand, I desperately wanted to return to my family on Earth. But on the other hand, I felt a strong urge to help Lika in her mission. The weight of my decision pressed heavily on me, and I knew there were no easy answers.

"I understand now, Lika," I said, my voice thick with emotion. "I understand why this means so much to you."

Lika nodded, her eyes meeting mine with a mix of gratitude and sorrow. "Thank you, Kenyzee. Whatever you decide, know that you have already made a difference by being here."

### *The Horrifying Truth*

Lika's voice grew quieter, filled with the weight of the memories she was about to share. "It wasn't until recently that I discovered the reason for my immunity. One of the members of G-Four Astral explained it to me. I am not well connected to the green core elements because I suffer from a condition that paralyzes half of my brain. I use a plant-based device to give instructions to my brain, which somehow protected me from the dark matter's influence."

The details of her story hit me like a tidal wave. The thought of losing everything, of watching your loved ones turn into monsters, was almost too much to bear. "I can't even imagine what you've been through, Lika," I said softly. "It's beyond anything I can comprehend."

## *The Burden of Survival*

The depth of Lika's pain was evident in every word she spoke, and I couldn't help but feel the weight of her experiences pressing down on my own heart. She had endured so much, faced so many horrors, and yet she remained determined to fight for the future of her world.

"The journey has been long and arduous," she said, her voice filled with emotion. "There have been times when I wanted to give up, when the weight of the loss and the responsibility felt too heavy to bear. But I kept going, driven by the hope that one day, we would find a way to stop the dark matter and restore balance to our world."

Her eyes met mine, and I could see the depth of her determination. "That's why your presence here is so important, Kenyzee. You have a unique connection to the core elements, and your abilities could be the key to saving our planet. But I understand if you need to return to your family. Your decision is your own, and I will support you no matter what."

The weight of her words pressed heavily on me, and I felt a deep sense of responsibility. "I understand, Lika," I said softly. "Your story has shown me the importance of this mission, and I will do everything I can to help."

### *The Resolve to Continue*

As I prepared to make my final decision, Lika's story stayed with me, a poignant reminder of the stakes and the sacrifices that had been made. The journey ahead was uncertain, but I knew that whatever path I chose, it would be guided by the lessons and the love I had encountered in this extraordinary world.

---

### *Turn To Chapter 11: Left Hand Side (Page no. 81)*

---

## Chapter - 11
# Developing Friendship with Lika

### *Shared Sorrows*

After hearing Lika's story, I felt an overwhelming wave of sadness. Her pain and loss resonated deeply with me, as I too often felt alone and misunderstood. The bond between us grew stronger, forged by our shared experiences of loneliness and sorrow. I looked into her eyes, seeing the depths of her struggle, and I knew I had to be there for her.

"Lika," I said softly, my voice trembling with emotion. "I promise you, I am here for you. You don't have to face this alone."

She nodded, tears glistening in her eyes. "Thank you, Kenyzee. Your support means more to me than you can imagine."

We embraced, holding each other tightly. In that moment, our connection deepened, and I felt a profound sense of belonging and purpose.

Later that evening, Lika and I decided to take a walk to a secluded place where we could find some peace and solitude. The green light creatures, with their soft luminescence, created an enchanting atmosphere. Their gentle, melodic sounds filled the air, providing a soothing background as we settled down to have dinner.

As we walked, I couldn't help but think about how our lives had intertwined so unexpectedly. Just days ago, I was lost in my own world of confusion and fear, and now I found myself drawn into a realm of otherworldly beauty and connection. The green light creatures danced around us, their bioluminescence casting a soft glow over everything. It felt like a scene from a dream, a moment of tranquility amidst the chaos of our lives.

We sat down in a small clearing, the soft grass beneath us a comforting cushion. The green light creatures flitted about, their gentle glow creating an almost magical ambiance. As we enjoyed our meal, I couldn't help but be mesmerized by the beauty of the surroundings and the serenity they brought. It was a stark contrast to the turmoil that had been consuming my thoughts and emotions.

Lika looked at me with a gentle smile. "It's beautiful here, isn't it?"

"Yeah," I replied, my voice filled with awe. "It's like nothing I've ever seen before."

She nodded, her eyes reflecting the same wonder. "This place has always been special to me. It's where I come to find peace and clarity."

I reached out and took her hand in mine, feeling a surge of warmth and connection. "Thank you for bringing me here, Lika. I needed this."

She squeezed my hand gently, her touch sending a comforting wave through me. "I'm glad you're here with me, Kenyzee. You've become an important part of my life."

## *A Tranquil Evening*

As we watched the green light creatures, I reached out and took Lika's hand in mine. Her touch was warm and comforting, and I felt a spark of something deeper between us. The connection we shared went beyond words, a silent understanding that we both needed each other.

"Lika," I whispered, my voice filled with emotion. "I don't know what the future holds, but I want you to know that I care about you deeply."

She looked at me, her eyes reflecting the same feelings. "I care about you too, Kenyzee."

Without thinking, I leaned in and gently kissed her hand. It was a tender gesture, one that spoke volumes about the growing bond between us. She smiled, her eyes filled with warmth and affection.

The atmosphere was charged with an unspoken worry, a mix of desire and connection that neither of us could ignore. I moved closer to Lika, my heart pounding in my chest. Our eyes met, and I could see the same longing reflected in her gaze.

I reached out and gently cupped her face, my thumb tracing the outline of her jaw. She closed her eyes, leaning into my touch. I leaned in and kissed her softly on the lips, a kiss that was filled with all the emotions we had been holding back.

The kiss deepened, becoming more passionate as our feelings took over. I moved my lips to her neck, kissing her gently near her ear. She sighed softly, and I felt her hands move to my shoulders, pulling me closer.

Driven by the intensity of the moment, I kissed her neck and moved my hands to her waist, pulling her even closer. Her skin was warm and soft under my touch, and I could feel her heartbeat quickening.

I kissed her again, this time more urgently, my hands exploring the contours of her body. I could feel the desire building between us, a powerful force that neither of us could resist. I kissed her near her ear, and she shivered with pleasure.

My hands moved to her breasts, gently caressing them as I continued to kiss her. She moaned softly, her breath hot against my skin. The world around us seemed to fade away, leaving only the two of us, lost in the intensity of our passion.

Our kisses grew more fervent, our bodies pressing against each other as we surrendered to the moment. I could feel the heat between us, the undeniable chemistry that had been building since we first met. It was as if all the barriers between us had dissolved, leaving only raw emotion and desire.

Lika's hands roamed over my back, her touch sending shivers down my spine. I could feel her responding to my touch, her body arching towards mine as our kisses became more urgent. The connection between us deepened, becoming something primal and intense.

In that secluded spot, surrounded by the gentle glow of the green light creatures, we lost ourselves in each other. The world outside ceased to exist, and all that mattered was the passion and connection we shared.

### *The First Touch*

As the intensity of our passion slowly subsided, we held each other close, our breathing ragged and hearts pounding. The moment left us both feeling vulnerable and exposed, but also deeply connected. We lay together, wrapped in each other's arms, basking in the afterglow of our shared experience.

"Lika," I whispered, my voice filled with tenderness. "I never want to lose this connection with you."

She smiled, her eyes filled with affection. "Nor do I, Kenyzee. You've become a part of me, and I cherish every moment we share."

We stayed like that for a long time, holding each other and reveling in the bond that had formed between us.

In that serene setting, I realized that my connection with Lika was more than just physical. It was a deep, emotional bond that gave me strength and purpose. Together, we could face whatever challenges lay ahead, and I knew that I was no longer alone in this journey.

The green light creatures' soft luminescence provided a soothing ambiance, making the evening even more magical. The tranquility of the moment allowed me to reflect on the journey that had brought me here, to this beautiful planet, and into the life of this incredible woman. Our connection was a beacon of hope in the midst of uncertainty.

## *Crossing Boundaries*

As the night deepened, we continued to share our thoughts and dreams. Lika told me more about her world, the struggles her people faced, and the beauty of their culture. I listened intently, captivated by her stories and the passion in her voice. She had endured so much, yet she remained strong and hopeful.

"I want to help you, Lika," I said, my voice filled with determination. "I want to be there for you and your people."

She looked at me with gratitude in her eyes. "You already have, Kenyzee. Just by being here, you've given me hope."

Our conversation continued, weaving a tapestry of understanding and connection. As we spoke, I felt a growing sense of purpose. My journey to Three Astral was more than just a series of visions; it was a call to action, a chance to make a difference.

Lika leaned closer, her eyes reflecting the soft glow of the green light creatures. "Kenyzee," she said softly, "I'm so glad you're here with me."

I smiled, my heart swelling with affection. "Me too, Lika. Me too."

We sat together, our hands intertwined, watching the green light tiny creatures as they danced around us. It was a moment of pure connection, a shared experience that transcended words. In that serene setting, I knew that we were bound by something deeper than circumstance—something that would endure, no matter what challenges lay ahead.

## *A Deepening Connection*

The intensity of our connection continued to grow as the night went on. Our shared experiences and emotions created a bond that felt unbreakable. The vulnerability we had shown each other allowed us to see each other in a way that few others ever could.

"Lika," I whispered, my voice trembling with emotion. "I never imagined I could feel this close to someone."

She smiled, her eyes filled with warmth. "Neither did I, Kenyzee. You've become such an important part of my life."

I reached out and gently caressed her cheek, feeling a surge of affection. "And you, Lika, have become a part of mine. I don't want to lose this connection."

She leaned into my touch, her eyes closing briefly. "You won't. We'll face whatever comes together."

Our conversation flowed naturally, each word deepening our bond. We spoke of our fears, our hopes, and our dreams for the future. Lika's presence brought me a sense of calm and clarity that I had never experienced before. The worries that had plagued me seemed to fade away in her presence.

As the night continued, we moved closer together, our bodies seeking warmth and comfort in each other. The green light creatures around us created a beautiful, serene backdrop that made the moment even more special. The soft, melodic hums they produced seemed to mirror the rhythm of our hearts, beating in unison.

## *The Strength of Our Bond*

The connection between us grew stronger with each passing moment. We were no longer two individuals facing our struggles alone; we were a team, united by our shared experiences and a common purpose. The bond we had formed was not just based on physical attraction, but on a deep emotional connection that gave us both strength and hope.

Lika leaned her head on my shoulder, and I wrapped my arm around her, pulling her close. "Kenyzee," she whispered, her voice filled with emotion, "I can't imagine going through this without you."

"You don't have to," I replied softly. "We'll face everything together, Lika. You're not alone anymore."

She looked up at me, her eyes filled with gratitude and affection. "Thank you, Kenyzee. Your support means more to me than I can express."

We sat there, holding each other, letting the peace of the moment wash over us. The green light creatures continued their gentle dance around us, their bioluminescence casting a soft glow that seemed to envelop us in a cocoon of tranquility.

As the night deepened, we found ourselves lost in each other, the world around us fading into the background. Our connection was all that mattered, a beacon of light in the darkness. We talked for hours, sharing our thoughts and dreams, our hopes and fears. Each word brought us closer together, solidifying the bond that had formed between us.

## Chapter - 12
## Training with Riko (Harmonizer)

### *Commitment to the Cause*

After spending a beautiful night with Lika, I felt a renewed sense of purpose and determination. Her story and the bond we had formed gave me the strength to face the challenges ahead. I understood that to help stabilize this planet, I needed to focus on all key core elements and try to connect with them. My main goal was to keep all core elements in their original place so that dark matter couldn't enter and destroy the stability of Three Astral.

For this mission, I needed to learn everything about the core elements and feel a deep connection with each one. Lika and I discussed our plan and decided that I should start my training with Riko, the master of the red core element and harmonizer. The journey to master the elements would be long and arduous, but it was a journey I was ready to undertake.

We woke up early the next morning, the soft light of the green core element casting a gentle glow over the room. Lika looked at me with a mix of pride and concern. "Are you ready for this, Kenyzee?" she asked.

I nodded, determination etched on my face. "I am, Lika. I need to do this for you, for Three Astral, and for myself."

We gathered our things and set off towards Riko's region. The journey was filled with anticipation and determination. Lika accompanied me, providing support and encouragement. The landscape changed dramatically as we traveled, transforming from the lush greenery of the green core region to the rugged, volcanic terrain of the red core region. The air was thick with heat, and the ground beneath us seemed to pulsate with energy.

As we approached Riko's domain, I felt a mixture of awe and trepidation. The area was dominated by towering mountains, rivers of molten lava, and the ever-present roar of volcanic activity. It was a stark reminder of the immense power that the red core element wielded.

Riko, the master of the red core element, was waiting for us at the entrance to his domain. He was a formidable figure, his presence radiating strength and authority. His eyes, like burning embers, assessed me as we approached. He stood tall and muscular, his skin a deep bronze that seemed to shimmer with the heat of the lava flows around us. His hair was dark and wild, and his expression was one of stern focus.

"Welcome, Kenyzee," Riko greeted me with a nod. His voice was deep and resonant, carrying the weight of someone who had mastered the element of fire. "Lika has told me about your mission. You have a long and challenging journey ahead of you, but I believe you have the potential to succeed."

"Thank you, Riko," I replied, trying to hide my nervousness. The heat from the lava flows was intense, and the air was thick with the smell of sulfur. "I'm ready to learn and do whatever it takes to help stabilize the planet."

Riko's expression softened slightly. "Good. The path you have chosen is not an easy one, but with determination and focus, you will find your way. Let us begin your training."

He led us deeper into the volcanic landscape, the ground beneath our feet crunching with each step. The heat was oppressive, and sweat began to bead on my forehead. Riko seemed unaffected by the extreme conditions, his movements fluid and controlled.

"To master the red core element," Riko began, "you must first understand its nature. It is a source of immense power, capable of both creation and destruction. You must learn to harness this power and control it with precision."

### *Embracing the Heat*

The first part of my training with Riko was to acclimate myself to the intense heat of the red core region. The heat was unlike anything I had ever experienced, searing and relentless. Riko explained that understanding and connecting with the red core element required not just physical endurance, but also mental fortitude.

"You must learn to embrace the heat, to let it flow through you," Riko instructed. "The red core element is powerful and volatile. It can be both a source of creation and destruction. To master it, you must become one with it."

Under Riko's guidance, I began a series of exercises designed to help me adapt to the extreme conditions. We started with simple tasks, like meditating near a lava flow and walking across heated ground. The heat was overwhelming at first, but Raijin's steady presence and encouragement helped me push through the discomfort.

Each day, we ventured deeper into the volcanic landscape. The ground was a mix of blackened rock and glowing magma, the air filled with the constant rumble of the earth. Riko would have me sit near a lava flow, the heat so intense that it felt like my skin was burning. I closed my eyes and focused on my breathing, trying to let the heat flow through me as Riko had instructed.

As the days passed, I began to feel a change within myself. The heat that had once felt unbearable started to become a part of me. I could feel the energy of the red core element coursing through my veins, filling me with a sense of power and vitality. My body grew stronger, more resilient, and my mind sharper, more focused.

Riko taught me to respect the power of the red core element, to see it not just as a source of destruction but also as a force of creation. He showed me how the volcanic activity could bring new life to the land, creating fertile soil for plants to grow. It was a lesson in balance, in understanding the dual nature of the element I sought to master.

### *Harnessing the Power*

With my body now accustomed to the heat, Riko moved on to the next phase of my training: harnessing the power of the red core element. This part of the training was both exhilarating and challenging, requiring precise control and unwavering focus.

Riko demonstrated various techniques for channeling the energy of the red core element. He showed me how to create and control flames, how to harness the power of molten lava, and how to use the element's energy to enhance my physical strength.

"The red core element is about intensity and passion," Riko explained. "It requires a strong will and a clear mind. You must learn to control your emotions and direct your energy with purpose."

I practiced tirelessly, pushing myself to the limits of my abilities. Riko had me perform exercises that tested my control over the element. One day, he had me create a small flame in the palm of my hand, holding it steady without letting it grow or diminish. Another day, he had me manipulate a stream of lava, directing its flow with my mind.

There were moments of frustration and doubt. The red core element was powerful and volatile, and there were times when I struggled to control it. But Riko's guidance kept me on track. He was patient but firm, always pushing me to go further, to dig deeper.

Slowly but surely, I began to master the techniques he taught me. I could feel the power of the red core element growing within me, becoming an extension of my own being. My movements became more fluid, my control more precise. The flames I created danced at my command, the molten lava obeyed my will.

One of the most challenging exercises was learning to enhance my physical strength with the red core element. Riko showed me how to channel the energy into my muscles, increasing my strength and speed. It was a delicate balance, requiring focus and control to prevent the energy from overwhelming me.

## *The Battle Training*

The final part of my training with Riko was the most demanding. He had prepared a series of challenges that would test my mastery of the red core element to its fullest extent. These challenges required not only skill and strength but also quick thinking and adaptability.

The first challenge was to navigate a treacherous path through a volcanic landscape, with molten lava flows and unpredictable eruptions. Using the techniques I had learned, I managed to create barriers of flame to protect myself and manipulate the lava to clear my path. It was a grueling test, but I emerged victorious, my confidence bolstered by the success.

The next challenge involved controlling a massive, raging inferno. Riko set a large area ablaze, and my task was to contain and extinguish the flames. This required precise control and immense concentration. I summoned all my strength and focused my energy, gradually bringing the fire under control and eventually extinguishing it completely.

The most intense challenge was the combat training, where Riko himself would be my opponent. This test would require me to use all the skills and techniques I had learned to date. The setting for this battle was a vast, open volcanic plain, with rivers of lava flowing through the landscape and the sky above filled with dark clouds of ash.

Riko's attacks were relentless, his control over the red core element masterful. I had to stay on my toes, using every ounce of my strength and focus to keep up. There were moments when I thought I might falter, but the determination to succeed pushed me forward. I created walls of flame to block his attacks, manipulated streams of lava to counter his movements, and channeled the energy into my strikes.

### *The Final Test*

The battle with Riko was unlike anything I had ever experienced. His mastery over the red core element was absolute, and his attacks came with a speed and intensity that left little room for error. Each strike was a test of my resolve, each maneuver a challenge to my newfound abilities.

Riko moved with the fluidity of the lava flows that surrounded us, his attacks swift and precise. He conjured massive fireballs, launched streams of molten lava, and created walls of flame to trap me. I had to think quickly, using the techniques he had taught me to defend myself and to counterattack. The heat was intense, the air filled with the roar of flames and the crackle of burning rock. My muscles ached, and my mind raced as I pushed myself to the limits of my abilities.

I focused on everything Riko had taught me. I created my own fireballs, hurling them back at him with all the strength I could muster. I manipulated the streams of lava, directing them to intercept his attacks and create barriers between us. The ground beneath us trembled with the force of our battle, and the heat was almost unbearable.

As the battle raged on, I began to feel a rhythm, a connection with the red core element that went beyond mere control. It was as if the element itself was guiding me, lending me its strength and power. I moved with confidence and precision, my attacks growing more powerful and my defenses more impenetrable.

In one particularly intense moment, Riko summoned a massive column of fire, directing it towards me with incredible force. I summoned all my strength, creating a shield of flame to protect myself. The impact was tremendous, the heat searing, but I held my ground. I pushed back, channeling the energy of the red core element into a powerful blast that dispersed the column of fire and sent Raijin staggering back.

"Well done, Kenyzee," Riko called out, a note of approval in his voice. "You have shown great progress. But remember, the red core element is not just about raw power. It is about control and balance."

I nodded, taking his words to heart. The battle continued, each moment a test of my abilities and my willpower. I could feel the energy of the red core element coursing through me, a powerful force that I had learned to harness and control.

### *A Newfound Strength*

With the completion of the final challenge, my training with Riko came to an end. I had gained a deep understanding of the red core element and learned to harness its power. The experience had transformed me, both physically and mentally. I felt stronger, more confident, and ready to face the challenges that lay ahead.

Riko approached me, his expression one of pride and approval. "You have done well, Kenyzee. You have proven yourself capable of mastering the red core element. Remember the lessons you have learned here, and use them wisely."

"Thank you, Riko," I said, gratitude and respect in my voice. "I will carry these lessons with me and use them to help stabilize Three Astral."

Riko nodded. "I have no doubt that you will succeed. Your journey is far from over, but you have taken an important step. Now, it is time for you to continue your training and learn about the other core elements."

Lika, who had been watching from a distance, approached us with a smile. "You did it, Kenyzee. I'm so proud of you."

I smiled back, feeling a sense of accomplishment and fulfillment. "Thank you, Lika. I couldn't have done it without your support."

With Riko's blessing, Lika and I left the red core region and set our sights on the next part of our journey. The training with Riko had been an incredible experience, and I knew that there were more challenges ahead. But with Lika by my side and the lessons I had learned from Riko, I felt ready to face whatever came next.

### *Preparing for the Next Challenge*

The journey back from the red core region was a time of reflection and anticipation. As we traveled, I thought about the lessons I had learned from Riko and how they would help me in my quest to stabilize Three Astral. The power of the red core element was now a part of me, and I was eager to continue my training with the other core elements.

Lika and I discussed our plans for the next phase of the journey. The next step was to train with Airi, the master of the blue core element. The blue core region was known for its icy landscapes and serene beauty, a stark contrast to the fiery intensity of the red core region.

"I'm ready to learn from Airi," I said with determination. "I need to understand the blue core element and how to connect with it."

Lika nodded in agreement. "Airi is a wise and patient teacher. I'm sure you will learn a lot from him. The blue core element is all about balance and stability, qualities that are essential for maintaining the harmony of Three Astral."

As we continued our journey, I couldn't help but feel a sense of excitement and anticipation. The training with Riko had been intense and challenging, but it had also been incredibly rewarding. I was eager to see what the next phase of my training would bring and how it would help me in my mission.

## Chapter – 13
# Learning from Airi and Mentor Tira

### *Arrival at Kori's Region*

As Lika and I journeyed deeper into the blue core region, the landscape transformed around us. The air grew colder, and the ground beneath us became covered in a thick layer of snow and ice. The trees and plants were coated in frost, creating a stunning, glittering landscape. The transition from the fiery red core region to the icy blue core region was stark, but it was a reminder of the diverse and interconnected nature of Three Astral.

Our breaths were visible in the cold air, and the chill bit through our clothing. Despite the cold, I felt a sense of warmth and determination within me. The journey had brought us closer together, and the bond we shared gave me the strength to face whatever challenges lay ahead.

As we approached Airi's domain, I couldn't help but feel a sense of awe. The landscape was dominated by vast glaciers, frozen lakes, and snow-covered mountains. The air was crisp and clear, and the silence was almost palpable. It was a world of ice and tranquility, a stark contrast to the fiery intensity of Riko's realm.

Airi, the master of the blue core element, was waiting for us at the entrance to his domain. He was a tall, imposing figure, his presence radiating a calm and steady power.

His eyes, the color of the deepest ice, seemed to pierce through me as we approached.

"Welcome, Kenyzee," Airi greeted me with a nod. "Lika has told me about your mission. You have shown great strength and determination in your training with Riko. Now, you must learn the ways of the blue core element."

"Thank you, Airi," I replied, "I'm ready to learn and do whatever it takes to help stabilize the planet."

Airi's expression softened slightly. "Good. The path you have chosen is not an easy one, but with patience and perseverance, you will find your way. Let us begin your training."

He led us deeper into the frozen landscape, the ground beneath our feet crunching with each step. The cold was biting, and every breath felt like inhaling shards of ice. Airi seemed unaffected by the extreme conditions, his movements fluid and controlled.

"To master the blue core element," Airi began, "you must first understand its nature. It is a source of immense power, capable of both creation and destruction. You must learn to harness this power and control it with precision."

### *Intense Training with Yuki*

The first part of my training in the blue core region was with Yuki, Airi's most trusted disciple. Yuki was a master of the blue core element, known for her precision and control. Her demeanor was calm and composed, but there was a fierce determination in her eyes.

Yuki led me to a frozen lake, its surface shimmering with a layer of ice. "To master the blue core element, you must learn to control it with your mind," she explained. "The blue core element is about balance and stability. You must find inner peace and focus your thoughts to harness its power."

The training was rigorous and demanding. Yuki had me sit in meditation by the frozen lake, the cold seeping into my bones. She instructed me to focus on the ice, to feel its energy and to connect with it on a deeper level. It was a test of mental fortitude and concentration.

"Clear your mind, Kenyzee," Yuki said softly. "Let go of all distractions and focus on the stillness within you. The blue core element is calm and steady. You must match its frequency."

I closed my eyes and took a deep breath, trying to clear my mind of all thoughts. The cold was intense, but I focused on the sensation, letting it become a part of me. Slowly, I began to feel a connection with the ice beneath me. It was as if I could sense its energy, its steady rhythm.

Yuki guided me through various exercises, each one more challenging than the last. She had me create and control ice with my mind, forming intricate patterns and shapes. The precision required was immense, and there were times when I struggled to maintain control. But Yuki's calm presence and encouragement kept me going.

One day, Yuki had me form a bridge of ice across the frozen lake, using only my mind. "Focus on the connection between your mind and the ice," she instructed. "Feel the energy flowing through you and direct it with precision. The bridge must be strong and stable."

I concentrated, feeling the cold energy of the blue core element coursing through me. Slowly, I began to form the ice bridge, extending it across the lake. It was a delicate process, requiring immense focus and control. My mind wavered at times, and the bridge would start to crack, but Yuki's steady guidance helped me regain control.

## *Advanced Techniques with Yuki*

As the days passed, the training sessions with Yuki became more intense. She introduced me to advanced techniques, pushing me to the limits of my abilities. One particularly challenging exercise involved creating a sphere of ice and maintaining its perfect shape while gradually melting and refreezing different parts of it. It was a test of precision and patience, and I struggled to maintain the delicate balance.

"Focus, Kenyzee," Yuki urged. "Feel the energy flowing through you. The core elements respond to your intentions, but you must be clear and focused."

The sphere of ice wavered in my hands, the surface cracking as my concentration faltered. I took a deep breath, trying to steady my mind and refocus my energy. Slowly, the cracks began to heal, the ice solidifying into a perfect sphere once more.

Yuki also taught me how to manipulate the temperature of the ice, a skill that required both mental and emotional balance. She demonstrated how to melt the ice partially and then refreeze it, creating intricate structures. The precision and control needed for this technique were extraordinary, and I spent hours practicing under her watchful eye.

Despite the challenges, I could feel myself growing stronger. The blue core element was becoming an extension of my own being, and I was learning to harness its power with greater skill and confidence. Yuki's calm and patient teaching style helped me push through my doubts and fears.

One day, Yuki set up a particularly difficult exercise. She had me create an intricate ice sculpture, a delicate and complex design that required perfect control over the element. As I worked, she offered guidance and corrections, helping me refine my technique.

"Remember, Kenyzee, the blue core element is about balance and precision. Every movement must be deliberate, every thought clear. Let the element flow through you, guiding your actions."

As I worked on the sculpture, I could feel the energy of the blue core element flowing through me. My movements became more fluid, my control more precise. The sculpture began to take shape, each detail perfectly formed.

Yuki watched with approval as I completed the sculpture. "Well done, Kenyzee. You are making great progress. Remember these lessons as you continue your journey."

### *Seeking Mentor Tira*

With the completion of my training with Yuki, it was time to seek the guidance of Mentor Tira, a legendary figure known for her profound understanding of the core elements. Tira was a recluse, living in the heart of the blue core region, and convincing her to help me was no small task.

Yuki accompanied me to Tira's dwelling, a secluded cave nestled within a towering glacier. The air was filled with an otherworldly glow, the ice reflecting the light in mesmerizing patterns. Yuki approached the entrance and called out respectfully, "Mentor Tira, we seek your wisdom and guidance."

For a moment, there was silence. Then, a voice echoed from within the cave, carrying a tone of both curiosity and authority. "Enter, Yuki, and bring the one who seeks to learn."

We stepped into the cave, the cold air wrapping around us like a cloak. Tira was sitting by a pool of glowing ice, her presence serene and commanding. She was an elderly figure, her eyes filled with the wisdom of ages. Her aura radiated a deep connection with the core elements.

"Who is this that you bring before me, Yuki?" Tira asked, her gaze piercing through me.

"This is Kenyzee," Yuki replied. "He seeks to master the core elements to stabilize Three Astral. He has shown great potential and dedication in his training."

Tira's eyes narrowed slightly as she studied me. "Why do you wish to undertake this journey, Kenyzee?"

I took a deep breath, feeling the weight of her gaze. "I want to help stabilize this planet and prevent the dark matter from destroying it. I have learned from Riko and

Yuki, but I need to understand the core elements more deeply to achieve this goal."

Tira nodded slowly. "Very well. Your journey will not be easy, but if you are truly committed, I will guide you."

### *Training with Tira*

Training with Tira was unlike anything I had experienced before. She had a profound understanding of the core elements, and her teaching methods were both rigorous and enlightening. The training sessions were intense, pushing me to the limits of my mental and physical endurance.

Tira began by testing my knowledge and skills, assessing my connection with the core elements. She had me perform various exercises, from creating intricate ice sculptures to manipulating the temperature and state of the ice. Her keen eye missed nothing, and she corrected my mistakes with precision.

"You must learn to see beyond the physical form of the elements," Tira instructed. "Understand their essence, their energy. The core elements are not just tools to be used; they are forces of nature that require respect and understanding."

Under Tira's guidance, I delved deeper into the mysteries of the core elements. She taught me advanced techniques for channeling their energy, combining mental focus with emotional balance. The exercises were challenging, requiring intense concentration and control.

One particularly difficult exercise involved creating a huge sphere of ice and maintaining its perfect shape while gradually melting and refreezing different parts of it. It was a test of precision and patience, and I struggled to maintain the delicate balance.

"Focus, Kenyzee," Tira urged. "Feel the energy flowing through you. The core elements respond to your intentions, but you must be clear and focused."

The sphere of ice wavered in my hands, the surface again cracking as my concentration faltered. I took a deep breath, trying to steady my mind and refocus my energy. Slowly, the cracks began to heal, the ice solidifying into a perfect sphere once more.

Tira also taught me how to manipulate the temperature of the ice, a skill that required both mental and emotional balance. She demonstrated how to melt the ice partially and then refreeze it, creating intricate structures. The precision and control needed for this technique were extraordinary, and I spent hours practicing under her watchful eye.

Despite the challenges, I could feel myself growing stronger. The blue core element was becoming an extension of my own being, and I was learning to harness its power with greater skill and confidence. Tira's calm and patient teaching style helped me push through my doubts and fears.

One day, Tira set up a particularly difficult exercise. She had me create an intricate ice triangle, a delicate and complex design that required perfect control over the element. The challenge was to form a hollow triangular shape with water encased inside, frozen at the apex. As I worked, she offered guidance and corrections, helping me refine my technique.

"Remember, Kenyzee, the blue core element is about balance and precision. Every movement must be deliberate, every thought clear. Let the element flow through you, guiding your actions."

As I focused on the task, I could feel the energy of the blue core element flowing through me. My movements became more fluid, my control more precise. The triangle began to take shape, each edge sharp and the water perfectly encased, frozen solid at the top. The sight was mesmerizing, a testament to the power and beauty of the blue core element.

Tira watched with approval as I completed the ice triangle. "Well done, Kenyzee. You are making great progress. Remember these lessons as you continue your journey."

The ice triangle stood before us, a symbol of my growing mastery over the blue core element. Each facet reflected the light, creating a shimmering display of colors. The water inside remained perfectly still, a testament to the control and precision required to create such a piece.

Tira smiled, her eyes filled with pride. "You see, Kenyzee, this is the essence of the blue core element. It requires a delicate balance, a harmony between thought and action. As you continue to train, remember this feeling, this connection. It will guide you through even the most challenging of times."

Her words resonated deeply within me. The creation of the ice triangle had been more than just an exercise; it had been a lesson in focus, patience, and the delicate balance required to harness the blue core element. As I stood there, gazing at the intricate design, I felt a renewed sense of purpose and determination.

## *The Struggle to Connect*

Despite my progress, there was a significant challenge that I could not overcome. I struggled to connect with all three core elements simultaneously. While I could harness the power of each element individually, merging them together in perfect harmony seemed beyond my reach.

During one particularly intense training session, Tira had me attempt to create a structure that combined the properties of ice, fire, and plant life. It was an exercise in balance and integration, but my efforts fell short.

The structure wavered and collapsed, the elements refusing to merge. Frustration welled up inside me, and I felt a deep sense of failure.

Yuki, who had been observing, approached with a look of disappointment. "Kenyzee, you must focus. The core elements require perfect harmony to work together. You cannot force them; you must guide them."

Tira's expression was stern, her eyes filled with a mixture of disappointment and determination. "Kenyzee, mastering the core elements is not just about control. It is about understanding their nature and finding the balance within yourself. You must be patient and persistent."

Despite their words, the feeling of inadequacy gnawed at me. I had trained tirelessly, pushing myself to the brink, yet I still couldn't achieve the harmony needed to merge the core elements. The weight of my failure felt overwhelming.

The days turned into weeks, and my struggle to connect with all three core elements simultaneously continued. Yuki and Tira were relentless in their training, each session becoming more challenging and demanding. Despite my best efforts, I couldn't achieve the harmony required.

During one particularly grueling session, Tira had me attempt to create a structure that required perfect balance and integration of the core elements. My focus wavered, and the structure collapsed in a spectacular failure. The frustration and exhaustion were evident on my face.

Tira's eyes narrowed with disappointment. "You lack the balance and inner peace needed, Kenyzee. You are trying to force the elements to your will instead of understanding their nature and working in harmony with them."

Yuki, who had been watching from the side, shook her head. "We had high hopes for you, Kenyzee. Your potential is undeniable, but your inability to connect with all three core elements is a significant setback. It's as if our efforts have been wasted."

Their words stung, and I felt a deep sense of failure. The weight of their disappointment was heavy, and I couldn't help but feel that I had let them down. Despite their frustration, I knew that their criticism came from a place of genuine concern and a desire for me to succeed.

*Three Astral: Thought's Deception*

I took a deep breath, trying to steady my emotions. "I understand your disappointment. I will continue to train and find a way to achieve the balance needed."

Tira's expression softened slightly. "Do not lose hope, Kenyzee. The path you have chosen is not an easy one. True mastery of the core elements takes time, patience, and a deep understanding of yourself and the world around you. Continue to search for that balance, and do not give up."

Yuki nodded in agreement. "We believe in your potential, Kenyzee. Do not let this setback deter you. Use it as motivation to push forward and find the harmony you seek."

With their words of encouragement, I felt a renewed sense of determination. The journey to master the core elements was far from over, and I knew that I had to dig deeper within myself to find the balance and harmony needed. The road ahead would be challenging, but I was ready to face it with newfound resolve.

As Lika and I prepared to leave the blue core region, I looked back at Yuki and Tira with gratitude. Their teachings had pushed me to my limits and beyond, and I knew that their guidance would continue to shape my journey.

"Thank you for everything," I said, my voice filled with sincerity. "I will not give up. I will find a way to achieve the balance and harmony needed to stabilize Three Astral."

Yuki and Tira nodded, their expressions a mix of pride and hope. "We look forward to seeing your progress, Kenyzee. Remember, the journey is just as important as the destination."

## Chapter - 14
# It Started

### *Return to the Greenion Region*

Lika and I returned to the Greenion region, our spirits slightly dampened by the realization that despite my progress, I still could not connect with all three core elements simultaneously. The lush greenery of the region seemed to mock my inability to achieve the harmony that was crucial for stabilizing Three Astral.

The familiar surroundings of the Greenion region should have been comforting, but instead, they only served to remind me of the monumental task still ahead. I had mastered the red and blue core elements individually, but bringing them together with the green core element remained an elusive goal. The weight of disappointment pressed heavily on my shoulders, and I could sense the growing doubt among those who had placed their hopes in me.

As we walked through the verdant landscape, the vibrant flora seemed to be thriving, unaware of the looming danger. Lika was silent beside me, her presence both a comfort and a reminder of the stakes. I glanced at her, hoping to find some reassurance in her eyes, but her expression was somber.

"I know you're trying your best, Kenyzee," she said softly, breaking the silence. "But we need to find a way to connect the elements. Our planet's stability depends on it."

"I understand, Lika," I replied, my voice tinged with frustration. "But it's not that simple. I can feel each element's energy, but merging them together... it's like trying to hold water, fire, and earth in my hands at the same time. They just won't stay together."

Lika nodded, her expression thoughtful. "Perhaps there's something we're missing. A piece of the puzzle we haven't found yet. Don't lose hope, Kenyzee. We'll figure this out together."

### *Disappointment and Doubt*

The days that followed were filled with a sense of unease. Despite my best efforts, I couldn't shake the feeling that I was failing those who depended on me. The pressure to succeed was immense, and the doubt in my abilities gnawed at my confidence.

Everywhere I went, I could see the effects of the planet's instability. The once-thriving ecosystems of the Greenion region were beginning to show signs of stress. Plants that had once stood tall and vibrant now seemed to droop, their leaves wilting. The air, usually filled with the sweet scent of blooming flowers, carried a faint hint of decay.

I spent hours meditating, trying to find the inner balance that would allow me to connect with all three core elements. But no matter how hard I tried, I couldn't achieve the harmony needed. The frustration built up inside me, a constant reminder of my perceived failure.

One afternoon, I sat by a tranquil stream, the sound of the flowing water offering a brief respite from my troubled thoughts. I closed my eyes and tried to focus, but the doubts kept creeping in.

"You have to believe in yourself, Kenyzee," Lika said, sitting down beside me. "I know it's hard, but you can't give up. The planet needs you."

I opened my eyes and looked at her, feeling a mix of gratitude and helplessness. "I just don't know how to do it, Lika. Every time I try to connect with all three elements, it feels like they're fighting each other. I can't bring them into harmony."

Lika placed a hand on my shoulder, her touch warm and reassuring. "Maybe it's not about forcing them together. Maybe it's about finding the common ground between them. They all come from the same source, after all. There has to be a way to unite them."

Her words offered a glimmer of hope, but the path forward remained unclear. The weight of my responsibility felt heavier with each passing day, and the doubt in my abilities continued to grow.

### *The Sound of Destruction*

One evening, a deep, rumbling sound shattered the tranquility of the Greenion region. The ground beneath us trembled, and I felt a sudden surge of fear.

"What was that?" I asked, my heart racing.

Lika's eyes widened with alarm. "It sounds like a mountain is collapsing. The instability of the core elements must be causing it."

Without another word, we ran towards the source of the sound. The ground shook beneath our feet, and the air was filled with the deafening roar of collapsing rock. As we approached, we saw a massive mountain crumbling, its once-majestic peak now a chaotic mass of falling debris.

I could feel the raw power of the core elements clashing, their energies out of balance and wreaking havoc on the planet. The sight of the destruction filled me with a sense of urgency and dread. This was the result of my failure to achieve harmony between the elements.

"Lika, we need to get closer," I said, my voice determined. "I have to try and stabilize this before it gets worse."

Lika nodded, her expression resolute. "Be careful, Kenyzee. The energy here is unstable and dangerous."

As we moved closer to the collapsing mountain, the ground continued to shake violently. I could see the energy of the core elements swirling chaotically, a visual representation of the planet's instability. The sight was both awe-inspiring and terrifying.

In the midst of the chaos, I saw Lika moving towards the epicenter of the destruction. My heart sank with fear. "Lika, no! It's too dangerous!"

But Lika pressed on, her determination unwavering. She was willing to risk everything to help stabilize the planet. The sight of her bravery filled me with a renewed sense of purpose. I couldn't let her face this alone.

## *Facing My Fears*

As I followed Lika towards the epicenter of the destruction, the fear and doubt that had plagued me were momentarily pushed aside. I had to focus on the task at hand and find a way to stabilize the core elements. The lives of everyone on Three Astral depended on it.

The air was thick with dust and debris, making it difficult to see. The ground was unstable, and every step felt precarious. But Lika's presence gave me strength, and I pressed on, determined to do whatever it took to save the planet.

"Lika, wait!" I called out, my voice barely audible over the roar of the collapsing mountain.

She turned to face me, her expression fierce and determined. "We have to do this, Kenyzee. We can't let the planet fall apart."

"I know," I replied, feeling a surge of resolve. "Let's do this together."

We reached the base of the collapsing mountain, the ground shaking violently beneath us. The energy of the core elements was palpable, a chaotic storm of conflicting forces. I could feel the power of the red, blue, and green cores clashing, their energies out of sync and tearing the planet apart.

I closed my eyes and took a deep breath, trying to find the inner calm needed to connect with the elements. I focused on the teachings of Riko, Yuki, and Tira, trying to bring the elements into harmony within myself.

"Lika, I need your help," I said, opening my eyes and looking at her. "We need to find a way to balance the elements together."

She nodded, her eyes filled with determination. "I'll do whatever it takes, Kenyzee. Let's stabilize this planet."

---

## *Turn To Chapter 13: Left Hand Side (Page no. 96)*

---

## Chapter - 15
# I Made It

### *Awakening to Urgency*

I awoke to the sound of Lika's voice, a mix of relief and urgency in her tone. "Thank you, Kenyzee, you came back to your senses," she said, her eyes reflecting both hope and fear. "However, we don't have much time. Everything in the Greenion region is being consumed by dark matter."

The gravity of her words hit me hard. I understood the importance of family and love more deeply now, having experienced the emotional turmoil on Earth. My connection to Lika and the planet intensified. As I listened, a wave of determination surged through me. I had to save this world.

The room around me seemed to pulse with the energy of the core elements, their presence a constant reminder of the stakes. The once-vibrant hues of the Greenion region were being overtaken by the encroaching darkness, and the weight of responsibility settled heavily on my shoulders.

### *The Transformation*

As Lika spoke, I felt a change within me. My eyes turned a brilliant green, my body took on a blue hue, and my hair ignited with fiery energy. The transformation was unlike anything I had ever experienced. It was as if my emotions were merging with the core elements themselves, amplifying my power and connection.

The sensation was overwhelming, a mix of pain and exhilaration as my entire being resonated with the energies of Three Astral. My senses heightened, and I could feel the pulse of the planet beneath my feet, the core elements calling out to me. I knew this was my moment to make a difference.

I remembered the countless training sessions with Riko, Yuki, and Tira. The lessons I had learned and the struggles I had faced all culminated in this moment. Using the depth of my emotions, I tried one last time to connect with all the core elements.

### *The Connection*

I closed my eyes and focused, reaching out with my senses to feel the frequencies of the red, blue, and green core elements. The world around me seemed to fade as I delved deeper into the connection. The pulsating energy of the elements flowed through me, and I began to synchronize their frequencies.

The process was intense, and I could feel the strain on my body and mind. But I persisted, drawing strength from the love and support I had felt from Lika and the urgency of the situation. Slowly, the frequencies began to align, resonating in harmony within me.

The energies of the core elements surged through my veins, their power almost too much to bear. My mind flashed back to the moments of training—Riko's fiery determination, Yuki's cool precision, Tira's unwavering guidance. Each lesson had prepared me for this, and I channeled their teachings into my efforts.

As the frequencies aligned, I felt a profound sense of unity with the planet. The core elements were no longer disparate forces but parts of a greater whole. The connection was unlike anything I had ever experienced, a symphony of power and harmony that resonated deep within my soul.

### *Stabilizing the Core Elements*

With the core elements' frequencies synchronized, I could feel their immense power coursing through me. I concentrated on stabilizing each element, guiding them back to their rightful places. The energy swirled around me, a chaotic dance that gradually transformed into a symphony of balance.

I visualized the planet as it should be, free from the encroaching dark matter. The core elements responded to my will, their energies settling into a stable, harmonious state. The ground beneath me stopped trembling, and the air grew calm. The planet's equilibrium was being restored.

The effort required every ounce of my strength and focus. The energies of the core elements were like wild, untamed beasts that needed to be guided into a state of balance. I could feel the resistance, the inherent chaos that threatened to overwhelm my control. But I held firm, my determination unwavering.

Slowly, the energies began to stabilize. The once-chaotic pulses of power transformed into a steady, harmonious rhythm. I could feel the planet itself responding to the change, the very fabric of Three Astral aligning with the restored balance of the core elements.

### *The Return to Normalcy*

As I continued to channel the core elements' energy, I could see the changes taking effect. The once chaotic landscape of Three Astral began to revert to its vibrant, life-filled state. The skies cleared, and the natural beauty of the planet shone through. There was no longer any space for dark matter to infiltrate.

The lush greenery of the Greenion region returned, the vibrant hues of the flora and fauna restoring the breathtaking landscape. The blue skies stretched endlessly, free of the dark tendrils that had threatened to consume the planet. The fiery mountains of the Riko region blazed with renewed vigor, their power harnessed in balance with the rest of the planet.

When I finally released my hold on the core elements, I felt a wave of exhaustion wash over me. The transformation receded, and I returned to my normal state. The silence that followed was profound, filled with the quiet hum of a world at peace.

I collapsed to the ground, my body trembling from the exertion. The calm and serenity of the restored planet contrasted sharply with the turmoil that had just been quelled. The sense of accomplishment was overwhelming, but it was tinged with a deep-seated worry. I had saved the planet, but at what cost?

## *The Loss*

As the calm settled, I looked around for Lika. My heart sank when I realized she was nowhere to be seen. I searched frantically, calling out her name, but there was no response. In the distance, I saw the dark matter region, a stark reminder of the danger that had threatened us all.

"Lika!" I shouted, my voice echoing across the now tranquil landscape. Panic gripped me as I realized she had ventured into the dark matter region. The realization hit me like a blow—she had sacrificed herself to ensure the planet's safety.

I fell to my knees, tears streaming down my face. The joy of saving the planet was overshadowed by the pain of losing Lika. The emotional turmoil was overwhelming, but I knew her sacrifice had given Three Astral a chance to thrive.

I screamed into the void, my voice raw with anguish. The dark matter region loomed ominously, a stark reminder of the price we had paid. The contrast between the restored beauty of Three Astral and the lingering darkness was almost too much to bear.

I felt a hand on my shoulder and turned to see Riko, Yuki, and Tira standing beside me. Their expressions were solemn, and I could see the pain in their eyes. They understood the gravity of Lika's sacrifice, and their presence was a silent testament to the bond we all shared.

## Turn To Chapter 16: Left Hand Side (Page no. 110)

www.ingramcontent.com/pod-product-compliance
Lightning Source LLC
LaVergne TN
LVHW041905070526
838199LV00051BA/2499